CRUMP

1600 Pennsylvania Avenue will never be the same again!

JP GUNBY

MAOS
Publications

Published by MAOS Publications

First edition

ISBN: 978-1-7329657-6-8

For Mum and Dad

More books by JP Gunby

The Adventures of Trumper Gallant and Bingo Malloy:

The Little Vampire of Counting House Lane

The Dragonbutt Itch

Contents

1   CRUMP   1

2   CRUMP on Elections   15

3   CRUMP on Guns   34

4   CRUMP on the Press   51

5   CRUMP on the Military   68

6   CRUMP on Religion   86

7   CRUMP on Education   103

8   CRUMP on Health   121

9   CRUMP on Climate Change   140

10   CRUMP on Pardons   158

11   CRUMP on Space   174

12   CRUMP'ed   193

1

CRUMP

"Fukkers, the lot of them!"
— Ronald S. Crump, President of the United States

* * *

As I apprehensively entered the Oval Office and stood before the famed Resolute desk holding a brand new notepad and my father's old ballpoint pen, I was not sure what fukkers the elderly man with the dyed blond hair had been referring to. However, over the next 12 months, I discovered that almost everyone was a fukker to the 47th President of the United States.

My name is Trenton Begby, and it was my first day on the newly established presidential internship program for international students. Having arrived from England only the day before, I was looking forward to learning everything I could from my mentor, the billionaire owner of Crumpburger, President Ronald S. Crump.

"Which one of those assclowns let you in here? They're going to be shitcanned when I find out who it was. Can't you see that

I'm getting my daily briefing from SHITE news. And why are you standing there with your mouth wide open? Are you a fukwit or something?" bawled Crump, as he turned away from the huge wall-mounted television that was playing his favorite news channel.

"No, Sir, I mean, Mr. President. I'm English. What I mean to say is that I'm Trenton Begby from England, and for the coming year, I'm going to be your intern."

"Trenton, my boy, of course, you are. Just call me Crump. All my friends do. I have a bunch of fuktards working for me that never tell me anything. If it was not for the fact that they make me look good, I'd shitcan every one of the fukkers," announced Crump, who leaned forward to shake my hand but made no effort to stand. "Well, back to the old grindstone. Take a seat so that you can listen to the briefing. When it comes to the news, I only ever watch SHITE."

Ronald Sherman Crump was a two-term president, and it was widely anticipated he would win the upcoming election to be the first person in over 80 years to call the shots for a third term. Under any other presidency, this would have been inconceivable due to the 22nd Amendment to the United States Constitution, which forbade any president from running more than twice. Famously, during the early days of his second term, the Crump-appointed Supreme Court had ruled that the Constitution was an ass, and therefore any amendments were declared null and void. This meant any sitting president could govern as he or she pleased, and so Crump proclaimed that for the rest of his presidency, he would rule by decree.

Calling him the 47th President of the United States was not entirely accurate because there were no longer 50 states in the Union as California had seceded at the end of his first term. In point of fact, it would have been somewhat more in keeping with the current state of affairs to dub him the President of the Former United States or even the First President of the Newfangled United States. Be that as it may, for the sake of continuity, Crump's closest advisors pleaded with him to leave his title unchanged to which he agreed and reportedly exclaimed in typical Crump fashion, "Who gives a fuk."

Although Crump inherited a chain of a dozen or so Crumpburgers scattered throughout the New York metropolitan area, it was not until the 90's that his business really took off. And it was no mere coincidence that he chose a young man from England to be his first intern as my home country had played a pivotal role in the creation of the immense Crump family fortune.

After hearing about the outbreak of mad cow disease and the subsequent ban on English beef, Crump immediately recognized that this was a business opportunity he just couldn't pass up. As infected cows were being slaughtered by the millions, he made the deal of the century to buy all the beef England could supply at only pennies on the dollar. With his product costs way down and profits skyrocketing, Crump was able to open Crumpburgers in every state of the Union. Then with his first billion safely hidden in an offshore bank, he made a deal with the government of India to supply enough mad cows to embark on Crumpburger's international expansion.

A bit of Bovine Spongiform Encephalopathy or BSE never hurt anyone, he had famously claimed in one of his now-deleted tweets. Though if truth be told, it did have unplanned side effects that were an altogether positive impact on his business. Initially, his customers found that every Crumpburger they ate resulted in no gain in weight, something his marketing team never failed to point out. Then a doctor from a small town in Indiana contacted Crump to say that he had discovered a marked reduction in brain function in Crumpburger customers. This was a worrisome development for Crump until his head of sales noticed that the dumber you are, the more Crumpburgers you eat, and just after that, mysteriously, the doctor disappeared.

"Let me tell you something, Trenton, and you should jot this down in that notepad of yours. I pretty much know everything there is to know, which is why I never read anything. Reading's for dumbfuks, and I can tell you that we have plenty of them working here. Now, I always start my day by sending at least a dozen tweets out before breakfast. Any shit will do, just as long as it confuses the hell out of those fukkers in the fake press and keeps them from assbadgering me. I then spend my mornings watching SHITE news because they always say good things about me. Of course, they're all a bunch of asslickers; all the same, if they keep on licking my ass and no one else's, then I'll tolerate the dickrattlers," declared Crump, who had become bored with SHITE news and was now flicking channels before finally settling on an episode of Scooby-Doo. "So what do you make of this place? I think it's a shithole myself, but the fukkers on the other side of that door tell me it has a history."

"Well, Crump," I replied, somewhat nervously. "It's certainly smaller than I was expecting, and compared to Buckingham Palace, it's downright poky. But all the same, I'm over the moon to have been given the opportunity to serve the Crump administration in the renowned White House."

"Ah, Buckingham Palace, now that's a residence more befitting a Crump. When I finish up here, I'm going to move to England and buy the whole enchilada from that Queen of yours. Naturally, I'll need to make a few alterations. As you know, it's prime real estate, so I'd build a humungous fukass Crumpburger out front," replied Crump, as he leaned back on his high back chair with a faraway look in his eyes. "And, Trenton, we no longer refer to this as the White House. I renamed the fukker, and so it's now officially called the Crump House."

The building housing the President of the United States, his family, and countless staff, had stood on the same spot for over two hundred years, and since 1901 had been universally referred to as the White House. More recently, to the annoyance of his neighbors, Crump had built an enormous drive-thru Crumpburger on the North Lawn bordering Pennsylvania Avenue. And although the structure remained a ghostly white, Crump had erected a large red flashing neon sign on the front of the building with the words, CRUMPBURGER – open 24/7, which could be seen for miles.

"Trenton, this is the best performing Crumpburger anywhere in the world. If that pissant fukker who sat in this seat before me had an ounce of common sense, he would have cut a deal with me long ago and made himself a killing. Knowing that I always make the right decision is what got me elected in the first place. That and lying to the bunch of dumb assholes who call themselves my base," chuckled Crump, as he stood up for the first time, revealing his tall yet rather heavyset body. "Crump knows best, and all those fukkers out there better believe it."

After dismissing all the presidents that preceded him as shitbrained fukbaggers that couldn't spot a good business deal even if it bit them on the ass, Crump went on to explain that for him, the presidency was all about making a fukload of cash. Following this, we had a two-hour lunch break that consisted of a mountain of Crumpburgers and half a dozen cans of diet coke, during which Crump proceeded to apprise me of his team of feckless Crump House staff. Then at two on the dot, there was a knock on the door, and in walked an attractive young blonde woman whose flirtatious smile made her look like she was one of those people who could speak faster than they can think.

"Ah, Tribianka, I was wondering when you would turn up. Trenton, this is my daughter and most senior advisor, the lovely Tribianka Crump. And Tribianka, this is Trenton Begby from England, my first presidential intern," said Crump, as he slapped both hands on his lap and called out, "Who's your Daddy?"

"You are, Mr. President," she squealed, while climbing onto Crump's lap and placing an arm over one of his shoulders. "It's so nice to meet you, Trenton. Daddy said that if I'm a good girl, he'll take me to England one day. Is it anywhere near Great Britain because I've always wanted to go there as well?"

"I think that's enough tough questions, for now, Tribianka. We don't want to tax Trenton too much on his first day at the Crump House, interrupted Crump, who was squeezing his daughter's thigh as he spoke. "Not counting the throngs of illegitimate money-grabbing fukkers that I've spawned over the years, Tribianka's the only one of my kids that has inherited my brains and good looks. And not only that, she's got a great ass to boot. Her brothers are just worthless fukwits, but I'm sure you'll meet those two imbeciles later."

At that moment, I was distracted by the sound of three feeble knocks on the door, and then a thin, pensive-looking man poked his head into the Oval Office, "Hi, Dad, is it alright if I come in?" Whether it was or not, the man did not wait to find out and marched right in carrying a pile of official-looking papers.

"No, it isn't, you dickfukker," yelled Crump, before throwing a Crumpburger at the man and hitting him on the lapel of his expensive tailored suit. "Trenton, remind me to have a sign nailed to the other side of that fukkin door stating, No Fukkers Allowed! And, Waywerd, I've told you a thousand times before to always call me, Mr. President. Now, what the fuk do you want?"

Waywerd Pushover was not only the Crump House chief of staff, but he was also Tribianka's husband, and that, to Crump's displeasure, made him his son-in-law. He was a sniveling wretch of a man that in the real world would have been nigh on unemployable. Luckily for Waywerd, he had been born into a family with tremendous wealth, and this had allowed his father, a two-time ex-con, to send him to the best schools he could buy off. Graduating from university with a 1.1 GPA and a bank account that was in the high eight-figure range, he appeared to be the perfect match for Tribianka. Unfortunately for Crump, like almost everyone else he knew, Waywerd turned out to be just enough useless fukker.

"Of course, Dad, I mean, Mr. President. It won't happen again, cross my heart and kiss my elbow. We've just heard that Fudrucker has won the Democratic nomination for President, which means he's running against you," babbled Waywerd, who was nervously forcing out the words as hurriedly as he could to address his autocratic father-in-law. "And that's not all; he's got the backing of the Posse."

"Obviously he's running against me, I'm the President and the Republican nominee, you fukbrained dickweasel. Smilin' Mo Fudrucker can blow my whistle and call me Sal. He's no match for Crump, but if we're not careful, this election could turn out to be one hell of a clusterfuk now that those fukjobs in the Posse are with him. Now get out of my office, and stay out," retorted Crump, to his cowering son-in-law who was wisely making a speedy exit. "Trenton, if I had left it up to that impotent fukker, I would have no grandkids at all."

"You mean to say that you're the father of Tribianka's children?" I gasped, with my hand on my forehead. "But is that legal?"

"As a matter of fact, I am. However, this is not Alabama, you know. I had to IVF every one of the cloned fukkers," winked Crump, as he gave the giggling Tribianka another squeeze on the thigh. "There must be 14 or more of them now, all perfect copies of yours truly, Ronald S. Crump. Mind you, I can never remember the names of more than three of them, but who gives a fuk is what I say."

Before Crump could elaborate on his success with IVF, yet another knock was heard at the door, and in stormed the Crump House press secretary, Bich Landers. Bich was the 28th person to hold the post of press secretary during the current administration and the only one to last more than two weeks. She was a stout woman with unremarkable looks and a southern drawl that sprung from her home state of Arkansas. Having never had real parents, and in true redneck fashion, Bich had grown up on a farm with her Granny, unsure which one of her eleven older brothers was her pappy. Thankfully though, she always went to great lengths to tell her own kids which of her brothers were their biological fathers.

"Ah, Bich, what can I do for you?" called out Crump, in an unexpectedly welcoming tone. "I hope those fukkers in the fake press are not assbagging you again."

"Howdy, Mr. President, It's about Mylo. He's gone and

knocked up another three Crump House interns," blurted Bich, who looked quite out of breath as she stood before Crump.

"That lecherous self-righteous fukker has got religion stuck so far up his ass that he refuses to wear a fukkin rubber. During my first term, we had to open an abortion clinic on the campaign trail just for him," fumed Crump, as he handed Bich a can of diet coke. "Trenton, you better write this down. Never forget to plug your funnel before you enter the tunnel."

Mylo Peckerhead was the Vice President of the United States and had been with Crump since the beginning of his run for the presidency. He was a confederate-loving evangelical and the former Governor of the great Crump-supporting State of Mississippi. The reason he was Crump's running mate in the first place was not that Crump ever agreed with Mylo or even liked him; in fact, it was widely known he couldn't stand the sight of the fukker. Nonetheless, the Crump campaign knew all too well that Mylo brought with him something worth its weight in gold, and that was almost every assheaded religious fanatic voter in the country.

"Mr. President, we can't afford to open up a can of whoopass by lettin' this fall into the hands of Smilin' Mo Fudrucker and those scrotelickin' Democrats. And if the fukkers in the fake press hear about this during an election year, it'll just be another fukkin news story for them to jerk off on. There's no choice other than to pay 'em off, just like the last lot of cumdumpsters Mylo knocked up," asserted Bich, while draining her can of diet coke.

"Bich, that's what the Republican Party election fund is for. Get in touch with Shifty Daniels, and he'll know what to do. Shifty's just started a 20 year stretch at Sing Sing, but he's still my personal attorney and the best fixer I ever had," responded

Crump, who out of boredom, was flicking through the channels on his television once again. "And tell that fukker, Peckerhead, to keep his dickbeaters off the interns or use a rubber next time. If not, he'll be spending the rest of the campaign locked up in the Halwell Jr. Institute for Horndogs at Rikers Island."

"Will do, Mr. President, I'll skedaddle along to my office right now and give him a call. And howdy, Trenton, I was grinnin' like a possum when I heard we had someone from England coming to work with us. Ya know, I've always had a hankering to visit the pyramids," hollered Bich, as she hotfooted her way out of the Oval Office as swiftly as when she had arrived.

No sooner than the Crump House press secretary had left, the phone rang on the Resolute desk. Then after half a dozen rings, nonchalantly, Tribianka answered it. As I watched her head nod repeatedly without uttering a single word, it occurred to me that the President's most senior advisor seemed ignorant to the fact that the person at the other end of the line could not see her. This went on for what must have been two or three minutes, then with a puzzled look on her face, she hung up on the caller and announced the boys were on their way.

"Goddamnit! Not those two assmonkeys again. Trenton, family are just a bunch of fukkers that you can never get rid of. And believe me, I've tried. Of course, that doesn't include you, Tribianka," winked Crump, who looked none too pleased his two sons were paying him a visit. "Before he kicked me out of the house, I learned everything I needed to know about family from my father. He despised the lot of us, especially my mother for giving birth to those fukwitted brothers and sisters of mine. I still remember the time when he said to me, Son, family will always let you down, but hookers never will. And he was right, you get what you pay for with a hooker, nothing more and nothing less, not like family."

As it turned out, Crump's father did get more than he paid for during one of his illicit liaisons in which he contracted an incurable disease from a street hooker named Cut-Price Val. However, Crump benefitted in the end because after a lengthy bout of madness, his father died at the age of 73 leaving him millions and sole ownership of Crumpburger. This meant, Crump proudly bragged, he inherited the fukkin lot, and his no-good mother and dipshit siblings received precisely fuk all.

"Trenton, I was always the clever one in the family. When my father fell ill, all the others just pandered to him by getting the best medical care money could buy. I was the only one who could see that he was a crazy fukker, and so I got him to make a new will leaving everything to me," sniggered Crump, as he helped himself to another can of diet coke. "Then, with some of my inheritance, I opened a bunch of homes for old fukkers and got Shifty Daniels to bribe a doctor to say my mother was as wacko as my old man. She's now living in one of them, and Trenton, this is the kicker, because she's got no money, the State of New York has to pay me for her fukkin stay."

Crump Retirement Palaces, or CRAPs, as they became known, were actually old rusty cargo ships that resembled prison hulks, which had been popular in the 18th and 19th centuries. He had bought them on the cheap from an acquaintance in the Russian government and then refurbished each of them in North Korea, to that countries highest standard. Then after sailing them around the southern tip of Africa, because he wouldn't pay the fee to cross the Suez Canal, Crump moored his CRAPs on major rivers throughout the good ol' US of A. And so with old fukkers packed in like sardines and the catering outsourced to Crumpburger, Crump, not surprisingly, was able to make another killing.

Hearing no customary knock, at that moment, the door to the Oval Office flew open, and in walked a bearded crossdresser followed by a man riding a tricycle. The crossdresser, I was about to find out, was Crump's eldest son, Ronald Crump Jr. He was wearing a Versace dress with an outrageously over-the-top floral pattern and smoking a foul-smelling pipe. Riding in circles as fast as he could around his older brother was Birk Crump, and although he was the youngest of Crump's three legitimate children, he was already 32.

"What do you two fukkers want? I'm a busy man with a country to rule," barked Crump, as he threw his last Crumpburger at Birk, while giving him the infamous Crump fukeye.

"I'm going to the Moon," cried out Birk, while waving his favorite teddy bear in the air.

"I wish that you would. And take that dickfuk of a brother with you," scoffed Crump, as he pointed to his other son who was emptying his pipe by tapping it on a bust of Winston Churchill. "Trenton, this is my eldest son, Ronald Crump Jr. He's got shit for brains and is currently running Crumpburger while I'm doing this gig as the leader of the free world. And every family has a moron, in our case, it's Birk. You know, before I was elected President, I never knew what to do with the witless fuknugget. Then when I found out that I could appoint any fukker I wanted, I gave him the job of heading up NASA."

In a rare moment of self-reproach, Crump confessed to me that he felt somewhat to blame for the state of Birk's brain. As a baby, he had given him to Tribianka to play with as she pleased, and like every other doll in her collection, she had spent her days dropping him on his head. Having been married four times so far, his children were the offspring of wives one to three. Wife number four, he went on to say, was the dumbest and biggest cumslut of them all, which, laughed Crump, suited him to a tee.

Seldom seen outside of the East Wing of the Crump House, Asyphilis Crump, the First Lady of the United States, was a mute Ukrainian pole dancer of some repute. Having slid down poles at almost every strip club in Eastern Europe, she garnered the attention of Crump, who brought her to the United States. Then after buying her an Einstein visa, which was reserved for only the most highly acclaimed people in their field, he divorced wife number three and married Asyphilis. Once they moved into the Crump House, Crump had a pole erected in the East Wing so that she could put her hard-earned skills to good use. And as a result, to her husband's delight, Asyphilis was able to entertain every lecherous visiting dignitary they received.

"Dad, according to marketing, Crumpburger hasn't been able to penetrate the juvenile market yet," remarked Ronald Crump Jr., who was snorting a line of coke on the Resolute desk as he spoke. "There's money to be made from those young'uns, and we need to get our hands on it."

"So what are you doing about it, you useless fukker? I didn't hire you to snort that shit all day and come bellyaching to me with fukkin problems," rebuffed Crump, who was now scrutinizing SHITE news to ensure they were giving him enough praise.

"Make them eat Crumpburgers, Daddy," squealed Tribianka, as she stood up and clapped her hands in glee.

"There you go. I knew my little girl would have the answer. Jr., if the fukkers aren't eating Crumpburgers, then make them," snapped Crump, while pointing his finger at Ronald Crump Jr. "What do you think, Trenton?"

"Have you ever considered offering smaller portions, and packaging them in boxes that appeal to kids?" I replied, as I was eager to make a good impression on Crump. "And maybe you could include a toy in the box to keep them occupied while their parents eat."

"Trenton, having you here is better than getting a wankjob by the Speaker of the House, and believe me, I've had plenty," chuckled Crump, with a dollar sign glinting in his eyes. "We can halve the size of our Crumpburgers and double the price. Jr., get marketing onto this right away and buy some cheapshit plastic toys from China. Better still, contact the Kims in Pyongyang and tell them that if they supply them for free, they can test-fire more rockets over South Korea. Oh yes, and Jr., let's add extra BSE and call them Little Fukkers."

"Daddy, I like little fukkers," giggled Tribianka, who had caught up with Birk's tricycle and was now rapping her knuckles on his skull.

"Of course you do, you're Daddy's little girl," grinned Crump, as he glanced at the time. "Well, that's enough work for today. Trenton, I'll see you again tomorrow, bright and early around midday. Tribianka can stay here, and Jr., if I don't see you and that dumbass brother of yours ever again, I'll be over the fukkin moon."

2

CRUMP on Elections

"Only lameass dicksticks lose elections. Crump always wins!"
— Ronald S. Crump, President of the United States

* * *

Two weeks had passed by since my first day at the Crump House, during which time Crump had spent his days playing golf and tweeting shit. But time waits for no fukker, he was fond of saying, and so today was the day Crump decided to convene his re-election committee. By now, I was brimming with confidence, and so clutching my notepad and pen, I gave a rat-a-tat-tat on the Oval Office door before boldly marching in.

"Fuknuts! Which of you dumbfukkers has come to chivvy my ass this time?" yelled Crump, who had been sitting at the Resolute desk aimlessly looking out of the window. "Ah, it's you, Trenton. I thought it was one of those fukkers from the other side of that door. Well, you've got perfect timing as usual because I'm just about to go on a live on-air call with the SHITE buddies. They're the best shitwaggers in the business, and naturally, they love a bit of Crump."

The SHITE buddies was not only the highest-rated show on SHITE news, but it was also the most-watched in the country with an average of 90 million viewers. It was hosted by the demented Vaj Ingersol, crackbrained Dicker Polson, and deranged 'Ranting' Prick Enderbee, who were all steadfast Crump supporters through and through. And due in no small part to the hosts ceaseless brown-nosing of all things Crump, which had ensured its popularity amongst Crump's base, Crump, rarely missed a show.

"Trenton, it looks like I'm on. Take a seat and listen and learn," announced Crump, as he leaned back on his chair, muted the television, and switched on his speakerphone. "Long time no see you bunch of cocksuckers. Prick, it's great to see you again with Dicker and Vaj. How was your vacation?"

"It's good to be back on SHITE news and talking with you again, Mr. President," acknowledged Prick, who was sitting on a sofa in the studio with his grinning SHITE buddies. "I had a whale of a time scuba diving and chasing after cheap ass tail in one of those shithole countries you told me about."

"I always knew that you were a badass, Prick. In those kinds of places, all you need to do is toss the fukkers a few dollars, and they'll treat you like a fukkin king," chuckled Crump, as he opened a can of diet coke. "Of course, the only diving I get up to these days is a little muffdiving, as Vaj knows all too well."

"Oh, Mr. President, that was supposed to be our little secret," cried out Vaj, who was visibly blushing at Crump's insinuation. "Let me hand you over to Dicker while I powder my nose."

"Dicker here, Mr. President. Now, what the whole country wants to know is how you feel about running against Smilin'

Mo Fudrucker?" asked the tight-assed Dicker, while giving Prick and Vaj a cursory glance.

"The sign out front says Crump, not Fudrucker, and I intend for it to stay that way. Smilin' Mo is just another fukkin Democratic dumbass," replied Crump, who turned around and gave me a thumbs-up and a broad grin. "I'll only give up the presidency when I'm good and ready, and that's not going to be until I've squeezed every last dollar I can from it."

"On behalf of my SHITE buddies, we wholeheartedly agree with you, Mr. President. The American people deserve Crump. Smilin' Mo Fudrucker and the Democrats could never measure up against you," declared Vaj, as she stood up and gave a salute to what I presumed had to be Crump.

"Mr. President, the Democrats claim that you only care about the one percent and that Fudrucker speaks for the downtrodden and voiceless in America," interjected Prick, who was reading from a teleprompter to stave off one of his trademark rants. "How do you respond to this accusation?"

"Firstly, Prick, I'll answer that by saying you should shit-can the dickwad who wrote that shitass mothafukker of a question. We should be talking about what matters to the Crump-supporting American public, and that's Crumpburger," snapped Crump, while throwing his empty can of diet coke at the television. "Prick, I'll tell you this for nothing, if you're not born a millionaire or have made your first million by the age of 25, then it's your fukkin problem, not mine."

"Well said, Mr. President, and that brings us to our last question. How is your new product line of Little Fukkers doing?" exclaimed Vaj, as SHITE news played a 30 second commercial of smiling children eating Little Fukkers.

"Just beautiful, Vaj, those goddamn fukkin ankle-biters can't get enough of them. It's the added BSE that makes them go crazy for more," laughed Crump, while turning his head to give me a wink. "Tribianka always orders a shitload of them for my grandchildren, and Birk eats nothing but Little Fukkers all day."

"As it should be, Mr. President, and it's always edifying and a privilege to speak with the finest leader the free world has ever known," proclaimed the SHITE buddies, as they waved Crump farewell while standing to attention.

"Trenton, if I don't say so myself, I believe that went pretty fukkin well. Every time the fukkers see me on-air with the SHITE buddies, Crumpburger sales go through the roof," grinned Crump, who was thinking this appearance must have made him at least a million. "Now, where's my Bich?"

"Great performance, Mr. President," hollered Bich, as she burst into the Oval Office with Oleander OnYurway in tow. "The SHITE buddies sure asked some tough questions, but ya answered them brilliantly. If this doesn't jack us up a few percentage points in the polls, then I'll change my fukkin name to Fanny."

I had met Crump's senior counselor, Oleander OnYurway, several times before. Although, as a top aide on the Crump House team, I still had no idea what her role entailed. OnYurway was originally from Russia and was rumored to have previously been employed as a hooker by Russian Intelligence. She was an intimidating-looking woman whose abrasive accent made the few words of English she spoke all the more difficult to understand. However, what I felt most disconcerting about Crump's senior counselor was the fact she always had a pair of .44 magnums strapped to her ample chest and holstered bandido style.

"So, Bich, I guess we better start this shitwaste of a meeting, and then I can get back to doing the real work, and that's making shitloads of money. Have you rounded up everyone in the team?" asked Crump, who was crushing an empty can of diet coke as he spoke.

"Your darn tootin' right I have, Mr. President. They're waiting over yonder in the Roosevelt Room," nodded Bich, while grinning from ear to ear.

Crump led the way with me by his side, and Bich and OnYurway followed only a few steps behind. In no time at all, we were taking our places around the large rectangular table in the Roosevelt Room with Crump at its head and Tribianka sitting bolt upright on his lap. In addition to Crump, Tribianka, Bich, and OnYurway, there was Waywerd Pushover and three others who I had not previously met. And blaring out of a speakerphone in the center of the table was the shrill voice of Vaj Ingersol.

"Alright Vaj, we're all present and accounted for so you can shut the fuk up," declared Crump, with a yawn. "Now, for you dicktossers that have forgotten, this is the first meeting of the Crump re-election committee to ensure that I continue my reign for another four years. And for those that have not met him yet, this is my presidential intern, Trenton Begby, from England. Trenton, I think you know everyone, except for Vaj and the three shitmeisters at the far end of the table. The big ugly fukker is Twatt Jabowsky. Twatt was the campaign manager for my first and second terms, and although he's a worthless pisshead, he's cheap, so I don't see any reason to replace him. The white-haired fukker to his right is our dirty trickster, Skeeter Shiznit. Skeeter's a devious fukster and not to be trusted, but he's the best in the business when it comes to dicktickling the fake press. And that brings me to the jerkoff in the corner; you may recognize him as my Vice President, Mylo Peckerhead."

"Ah, you're from the dear old blessed Isle. You know that my ancestors came from England, and so did our Lord Jesus Christ," chimed in Mylo, who was fondling the crucifix he was holding in his hand. "The Peckerheads sailed on the Mayflower all the way to these heathen shores to spread the word of God. And I'm heartened to say that this Peckerhead has continued their work by serving the new Messiah, Ronald S. Crump."

"Mylo, you're nearly as good a shitwagger as Vaj and the other SHITE buddies. Just keep spouting that religious claptrap of yours and the evangelical votes will come rolling in," commented Crump, while giving me an approving nod as I jotted down his words in my notepad. "Now, I'll hand the meeting over to Twatt so that I can get some well-deserved shut-eye."

"Thank you, Mr. President. First on my agenda is the polling numbers," announced Twatt, before taking a slug of Kentucky moonshine from a large ceramic jug he had brought with him. "We're leading Fudrucker in the polls, but he's starting to gain ground, and that rankles me like a corncob up the ass."

I had read that the US of A was roughly split 40-40 into Republican Crumpers and Democratic never-Crumpers, with the other 20% noncommittal. However, after the secession of California, this had shifted the political landscape in Crump's favor. Crumpers were typically gun-toting SHITE news watching high school dropouts with an IQ of <100, and, of course, they were voracious consumers of Crumpburgers. Never-Crumpers, on the other hand, had jobs and paid taxes. Then there was the undecided 20% who were considered somewhere in-between. Although because of the growing popularity of Crumpburger, most had backed Crump to give him landslide wins at the last two elections.

"It's the swing states of Florida and fukkin Texas that are making me scratch my scrote. Even though Crumpburgers are selling by the assload down there, they have too many undecideds and never-Crumpers moving in," warned Twatt, as he took another gulp of moonshine. Then he wiped his mouth on the sleeve of his shirt before passing the jug around the table. "The intel we're getting is that the undecideds and never-Crumpers look upon you as an elitist, Mr. President, and they regard Fudrucker as a man of the people."

"Of course, I'm an elitist, you dicksneeze. Crumpers, never-Crumpers, or undecideds, they're goddamn shitshovelers the lot of them. I wipe my ass on $100 bills and only hang out with the rich and famous, roared Crump, who was clearly not happy with what he had heard. "So, Twatt, what do you propose to do about it?"

"Dad, I've got an idea," called out Waywerd, while feebly waving his hand in the air.

"Fuksucker! I forgot that you were here," grumbled Crump, as he shook his head from side to side while giving his son-in-law the fukeye. "Waywerd, it's, Mr. President, and this better be good. And put your hand down, you look like one of those pussyfooting dickswingers in the Democratic Party."

"Sure, Dad," replied Waywerd, who was usually not the sort of person to have ideas. "Why don't we invite the press into the Crump House so that they can see firsthand what an everyday all-American family the Crumps really are? There's no way anyone will call you elitist after that."

"The SHITE buddies would be honored to do an exclusive report from the Crump House, Mr. President," broke in Vaj, from the SHITE news studio. "Never fear, we'll stick it to those fukkers that are too dumb to know Crump is the only one who can rule this beloved money-loving nation of ours."

"Um, what do you think, Twatt?" asked Crump, as he sipped his diet coke.

"It could work, Mr. President, but we'll need to invite the fake press," answered Twatt, while wrestling his jug of moonshine away from Bich.

"My brother Cooter says that it's always best to keep it in the family. And everyone around this table knows that's SHITE news," challenged Bich, who was all riled up after taking 3 slugs of moonshine back-to-back. "When I was on the farm in Arkansas, we all listened to Cooter. He's the pappy of two of my young'uns and the only one in the family to finish elementary school."

"Mr. President, if we only allow SHITE news to spend time with your family, putting it bluntly, it'll look like a fukover. For this to work, we're gonna need some of those fukkers in the fake press to cover this story too," asserted Twatt, while guzzling more moonshine.

After having a few words with Tribianka, during which time the rest of us had to turn our backs, Crump agreed to not only invite the SHITE buddies into the Crump House but the fake press as well. As she was never one to handle strong liquor, this led to a profanity-laden outburst from Bich comprising words that even Crump had never heard before. However, this lasted only as long as the time it took for OnYurway to lean across the table and slap the Crump House press secretary across the face. And then kicking and cussing, she dragged Bich from the room.

"Moving on, Mr. President, the second item on my agenda concerns Fudrucker's running mate, the Democratic vice presidential nominee," announced Twatt, after OnYurway had returned to the Roosevelt Room and taken her place at the table. "I know this is going to be a pisser, but we've just heard that he's chosen to run with LSD."

"LSD! That nagass fukker, she's nearly as big a jagoff as Mylo here," bellowed Crump, as he pointed to the Vice President. "I've refused to speak with her ever since the House tried to impeach me. Twatt, she's just a goddamn bitchass peacher."

"Daddy, I don't like peaches," uttered Tribianka, who was lacking her usual asinine smile when she spoke.

"See, Tribianka doesn't like her either," snapped Crump, as he threw his empty can of diet coke at Twatt.

All anyone knew about LSD were her initials and the fact that she was the most prominent member of the notorious Posse. According to Crump, the Posse were four Democratic Congresswomen from shithole countries who had come to prominence early on in his second term of office. LSD and her three congressional compatriots were the ones behind Crump's impeachment some two years prior because of his insistence that he had the right to rule by decree. Although, as it turned out, peachment by the assweasels in the Democratic-control led House amounted to no more than a bag of shit, so Crump bragged to me, as he said the fukkers in the Senate and Supreme Court were all bought and paid for by him.

The unyielding Posse had become a force to be reckoned with since Crump's awkward impeachment. And if their support for Smilin' Mo Fudrucker had not been sufficiently worrying, the news of the sharp-tongued LSD entering the race had now invoked Crump's wrath. Crump was already all too aware that LSD was more than a match for the assbrained Mylo Peckerhead. And he knew that if the fukheads in his team were not careful, the swing states might just be pushed from beautiful Republican red to shitster Democratic blue. However, before Crump could vent his ire on Twatt and the rest of the re-election team, someone could be heard tapping on one of the windows of the Roosevelt Room.

"What the assfuk is Bich doing out there?" demanded Crump, while pointing to his press secretary. Who at that moment appeared to be swinging from a branch of a tree.

"I'll save her," shrieked Waywerd, who leaped from his chair and was opening the window before anyone could stop him.

It could not have been more than a second or two after the first of the high-pitched sirens went off throughout the Crump House that Bich swung through the open window. With Waywerd cowering face down on the floor and the rest of us diving for cover under the table, half a dozen of Crump's handpicked Secret Service agents burst into the Roosevelt Room and discharged their weapons. Then more agents followed and grabbed Crump before bundling him off to the presidential bunker, but not before pushing an indignant Tribianka to the floor.

After the gunfire had ceased and seeing that they had hit just about everything in the room except their intended target, the agents pulled out their tasers. One hit Waywerd, and another two found Bich before she called out, "Heavens to Betsy, fellas, hold your horses. It's just me, little ol' Bich."

Realizing they had just tasered the Crump House press secretary and its chief of staff, not to mention shooting up the Roosevelt Room, the Secret Service agents holstered their weapons and stood down. While Bich looked hyped-up and was excitedly shaking her fists in the air like she was on some sort of sugar rush, Waywerd was unconscious and had to be stretchered out of the room with Tribianka by his side. Then after the all-clear was called and an announcement made informing everyone in the building that it had been another false alarm, we were told the meeting would reconvene in the Oval Office.

"Sorry about that, Mr. President. Ya know how I get when I'm liquored up on hooch," blurted Bich, as we marched into the Oval Office to see an annoyed-looking Crump sitting with his arms folded at the Resolute desk.

"Bich, when it comes to tempting trouble, you're a real shitmagnet," barked Crump, while giving her the fukeye as he opened a can of diet coke. "And what the fukwag were you doing up a tree in the first place?"

"Well, it was like this, Mr. President. After I was kicked out of the meetin', the Secret Service told me I wasn't allowed back in. That's when I pinned back my ears at the keyhole and heard all about how LSD is runnin' for Vice President. So I went out back and shinnied up the closest tree to get ya attention," explained Bich, with a grin. "Back in Arkansas, all us gals are taught to climb before we can crawl. As Granny often says, if ya don't want a young'un before the age of 12, then ya better learn to climb a tree."

"The Secret Service is none too pleased that you fukked-up two of their agents. And that's not the first time you've put them in the hospital," lectured Crump, who was pointing one of his fingers directly at Bich. "Trenton, this sort of thing happens every few weeks, so you better get used to it. We've lost more agents within these walls over the past seven years than all the previous administrations put together. Oh well, there are plenty more fukkers lining up for their pitiful jobs, so what the hell. My only regret is missing that shitwit, Waywerd, getting his ass tasered, although it doesn't seem to have done you any harm, Bich."

"It felt just like a horny raccoon was ticklin' my ass," giggled Bich, as she sat down on a chair while the rest of us parked ourselves on the sofa. "Mr. President, don't ya think that it's about time we got OnYurway to send that coochass fukker, LSD, on her way, if ya know what I mean."

"Of course I know what you mean, but LSD is not one of the fukkin fake press. You can shoot those fukkers all you want and no one will give dickshit. In fact, you'll probably be awarded a medal," replied Crump, who was calling Vaj Ingersol so that she could join the meeting again via speakerphone. In the meantime, I saw that OnYurway was fingering her magnums while giving Crump a badass-style smile. "Now, do any of you good for nothing dickslappers have any more ideas that pertain to me winning this election?"

"Mr. President, praise the good lord that you're safe and unharmed," yelped Vaj, all of a sudden. "We've been broadcasting for the past 30 minutes the story that you single-handedly fought off a crazed and heavily armed Fudrucker supporter who had broken into the Crump House. Prick is on-air now and ranting about it while Dicker is interviewing Tribianka and Waywerd Pushover, whose lives you heroically saved. We'll spit the shit on this story for as long as we can, and if any of those fukkers in the fake press discovers the truth, then SHITE news will simply claim they're spreading fake news again."

"Excellent, Vaj, I know that I can always rely on the SHITE buddies to stand behind me by making up shit," attested Crump, who was now looking at his Vice President. "So, Mylo, you kissassin waste of space, what do you think we should do?"

"God is on our side, Mr. President, and so I will leave

everything to him," professed Mylo, while holding up his crucifix for us all to see.

"Assbag! I don't trust any fukker who's not on the payroll," scoffed Crump, as he slammed his fist down on the Resolute desk. "You'll have to do a lot better than that now LSD is Fudrucker's running mate. If not, she's going to make you look like a class A cockbite by flailing your ass all the way back to Mississippi. Twatt, what have you come up with?"

"We've got you speaking at rallies from now until the election, Mr. President. And as you know, you can shitwag anything you like to Crumpers, and the jackasses will believe every word you say," answered Twatt, who took another slug of moonshine before elaborating further. "The Republican Party election fund and the taxpayers are paying for everything, so the rallies aren't going to cost us a fukkin dime. Naturally, we'll still claim them as a tax deduction, and we're sure to make a crapload from merchandising and Crumpburger sales at each venue."

"And what are the entrance fees for the fukkers this year?" inquired Crump, as he was eager to make this election the most profitable yet.

"Standing is $25, seating is $50, and for $100 we've got a VIP section that we're calling, The Trough. You get a seat, an autographed photo of you, Mr. President, and all-you-can-eat Crumpburgers for the duration of the event," responded Twatt, who was tapping his empty jug as he spoke.

"I want you to double the price of everything, Twatt. Trust me, those fukkers will pay anything to hear me speak, and so let's fleece their asses for as much as we can," proclaimed Crump, with an artful-looking grin. "Now, Skeeter, you've been as useful as a limp fukstick this afternoon. What do you have planned?"

"Mr. President, I'm going to be stirring up the shit on Fudrucker and LSD and then leaking it to the press," shared Skeeter, who had been quietly vaping on buds for most of the meeting. "SHITE news is running a story over the next week that labels Smilin' Mo Fudrucker, the Christian hating Prince of Darkness. Obviously, I made it up, but if we keep repeating the same story for long enough, even the fukkin never-Crumpers will believe it. And I'm now talking with Dicker Polson about an exclusive that claims LSD is really a Canadian lumberjack and ex-con named Louis Sacrament DuPre, or Big Louis as we've nicknamed her."

"Sounds like your balls are on the job, Skeeter," laughed Crump, as he leaned back on his chair. "Right, that's enough work for me today. Trenton, you stay here, and the rest of you can fuk off while I go for a quick wazz in the presidential bathroom."

It was not until the following month that selected members of the press were allowed unfettered access to the inner sanctum of the Crump House, which included both the West and East Wings and the Crumps' living quarters in the Executive Residence. Along with Vaj Ingersol from SHITE news, Bich had invited two reporters from the fake press representing the Democratic News Network and the Socialist Broadcasting Company. Crowded into the Oval Office were not only Crump, Tribianka, Bich, OnYurway, and myself, along with Vaj Ingersol, Raz Alvarez of DNN, and Stoner McCall from SBC, but also Arkansas's only professional football team, the Little Rock Hyenas.

Though the Hyenas had never won the Super Bowl, and over the past two decades had failed to win even a single game, Crump had decided they should receive the Presidential Medal of Freedom. The reason for this was that their owner, Buford P. Bucksnort, was a top donor to Crump's campaign and the proprietor of a dozen Crumpburger franchises throughout the State of Arkansas. And of course, it had been Bich's idea, as a wannabe Hyena cheerleader during her younger days, to invite the press into the Crump House on the same day as the ceremony.

Once the formalities were over, and the obligatory photos had been taken, Crump helped himself to a can of diet coke and then turned on the television for an afternoon of channel hopping. At which point, the rest of us were split into two groups before marching out of the Oval Office. The Hyenas accompanied Tribianka to the Executive Residence, and Bich, OnYurway, and I escorted the members of the press on a tour of the West Wing and then onto the offices of the First Lady.

Upon entering the East Wing, we were nearly run over by Birk on his tricycle, who, as usual, was yelling, "I'm going to the Moon." Even though I had become accustomed to the oddities of Crump's youngest son, I could not help but notice that he had taped a large cylindrical container to the back of his tricycle. And to my alarm, it had the words, Rocket Fuel, written down one side. It was during this kerfuffle that Stoner McCall gave Bich and OnYurway the slip so that he could go on a tour of his own choosing, and that turned out to be the Executive Residence. Then after conveying my concern to Bich about what I had just observed, she brushed it off as of no consequence and told the remainder of our group we should forge on.

Ronald Crump Jr. was sitting at his desk with a mountain of coke to his left and three lines in front of him, which quickly disappeared up his nose by way of a $100 bill when he heard us walking into his office. I could see that he had made quite an effort to dazzle our guests by wearing a black sequined ball gown and a hot pink wet-look lipstick that was clearly there to impress. With his eyeballs bulging, the head of the Crump family business sniffed and pinched his nose before standing and greeting the two remaining members of the press. Then after a quick round of photos, he stuffed a pipe with his favorite Afghani blend tobacco before accompanying us to Asyphilis Crump's much-celebrated pole dancing studio.

Within minutes we were standing before an impressive set of arched double doors which Ronald Crump Jr. flung open without a moment's hesitation. Then after lighting his pipe with a 24-karat gold lighter, he smiled and brashly waltzed in. Before the rest of us could follow, I heard three rings of a bell and then the all too familiar words, "I'm going to the Moon." What came next was somewhat confusing, but I do remember seeing Birk on his tricycle race past me, and then a flash of light and a loud bang before my own lights abruptly went out.

Somewhat dazed, I woke up on the sofa in the Oval Office, unsure how I had got there. Then I noticed a despondent-looking Bich and OnYurway standing before Crump and slowly nodding their heads. Once the three of them saw that I was conscious, Bich explained that most of the East Wing had been destroyed by a terrible explosion. And while the cause of this was still under investigation, all the evidence pointed to Birk whose canister of rocket fuel must have ignited after its fumes came into contact with the smoldering tobacco in his brother's pipe.

In fact, the only part of the East Wing that remained were the outer walls, sections of the roof, and Asyphilis's greased pole, which, surprisingly, was still standing. And while there had been no fatalities, the First Lady was in a state of shock, and after two hours of frantic searching, Birk had yet to be found. Ronald Crump Jr., on the other hand, to Crump's disappointment, had come out of this ordeal relatively unscathed, aside from a pair of singed eyebrows, a ruined ball gown, and the loss of his precious nose candy.

"Ah, it's good to see you back on your feet, Trenton, and with no permanent damage, I hope," said Crump, as he walked over to the sofa and slapped me on the back. "Bich, what I want to know is who the fuk allowed Birk to get his hands on rocket fuel of all things?"

"That'd be you, Mr. President, when ya made him head of NASA," answered Bich, who was browsing through the messages on her phone as she spoke. "Mr. President, there's been a development with Birk. Ya should switch channels to DNN because ya sure gonna want to see this."

Just then, the door to the Oval Office flew open and in stomped Tribianka, who cried out, "Daddy, I think I've been a naughty girl again."

"Not now, Tribianka, Daddy's got to watch something on the television," smiled Crump, while switching from SHITE news to DNN and turning up the volume.

With her head bandaged and a suspected fractured arm, Raz Alvarez had sought only the bare minimum of medical treatment before jumping into the DNN helicopter. While surveying the extensive damage the explosion had caused to the Crump House, she spotted a bizarre sight on top of the 555-foot marble obelisk known as the Washington Monument. Circling the famous landmark, Raz was now giving a live on-air report to the 25 million DNN news viewers, and for once, one of them was Crump.

"This is Raz Alvarez reporting live from the DNN helicopter

in the skies above our nation's capital. Earlier this afternoon, I was nearly killed when a blast ripped through the East Wing of the Crump House. Although we have received no details from President Crump's team regarding any casualties or the cause of this explosion, I can confirm the whereabouts of his youngest son, Birk Crump. Birk appears to be sitting on a tricycle on top of the Washington Monument, and I believe he is trying to communicate with us. Yes, we're picking up his words now, and it sounds like he is calling out, I'm going to the Moon."

"Asshead! If that fukwit thinks I'm going to rescue him then he's got another thing coming," exclaimed Crump, who was shaking his head. "Bich, the fukker can stay up there, and if his mother calls to complain, then tell her that I'll have the US Air Force shoot the dickstain down."

"Righty-oh, Mr. President, but there's more ya gotta see. Ya better take a look at SBC because they're spoutin' all kinds of horseshit," stressed Bich, as she changed channels just as Stoner McCall came on-air for the second time in the past half hour.

"You're watching Stoner McCall live in this SBC exclusive from the grounds of the Crump House. I witnessed two bangs this afternoon and am not sure which was the most shocking. The explosion that demolished the East Wing or the gangbang in the Executive Residence involving Tribianka Crump and the Little Rock Hyenas..."

"Goddamn shitdiggers. I've got a good mind to order the Secret Service to shoot every one of those fukkers," fumed Crump, as he slammed his fist down on the Resolute desk.

"It wasn't the whole team, Daddy. It was only the starting lineup," whined Tribianka, who was now sitting on Crump's lap.

"There, you go, fake news again. The fukkers are just a bunch of shitbreathing asswipes," yelled Crump, while giving Tribianka a reassuring squeeze on the thigh.

"I warned ya about the fake press, Mr. President. Whenever the fukkers get the chance, they'll assjab ya every time. We should have stuck with SHITE news," chimed in Bich, who was getting all riled up again.

"Bich, you better get me on the SHITE buddies tomorrow morning so that I can shitwag this train wreck of a fukup," instructed Crump, as he opened another can of diet coke. "And Bich, the next time Waywerd has an idea, I want OnYurway to shoot the lameass fukker in the head."

3

CRUMP on Guns

"Guns are for assholes. But if the fukkers vote Crump, then I'm all for them!"
— Ronald S. Crump, President of the United States

* * *

After the debacle with the fukkers in the fake press, Crump chose to spend the next three weeks at Kiss-my-Ass, his private members-only club and luxury island resort in the Caribbean. Accompanying him were the First Lady, Tribianka, Bich Landers, and Oleander OnYurway, and I was cock-a-hoop that he had invited me along as well. And though Crump didn't actually do an ounce of real work during the duration of our stay, his tweets went into overdrive while teaching me a thing or two about the art of doing business the Crump way.

Only lamebrained fukkers pay taxes, Crump told me on an exceptionally sultry afternoon. And that was why he had built Kiss-my-Ass on a tax-free haven off the coast of Mexico. In a cashless deal with the Nachos Cartel, Crump had purchased the whole island lock, stock and smoking barrel, and that included its inhabitants numbering a little over 200. While the Nachos family received exclusive rights to distribute their product at every Crumpburger south of the border, Crump gained valuable real estate at no cost to him. Then as Crump was always hungry to make an extra buck, he shipped every resident of the island to a Crump-owned detention facility in North Dakota. And naturally, this was at the American taxpayers' expense.

"It's back to work again, Mr. President," declared Bich, who was sitting across the table from Crump as we flew back to Washington, DC aboard Air Force One. "Skeeter's done a whoopass job while we've been away because the whole shittin' country has been talkin' about Fudrucker and askin' if he really is the goddamn devil. As we anticipated, the dumbasses have pretty much forgotten about what went down at the Crump House, so that's helpin' us move up in the polls. He wasn't so successful with LSD though. The Justice Department tried to have her extradited to Canada, but the dickbrained Canadians wouldn't take the bichmonger. I can tell ya that she was madder than a fukkin wet hen, so that's some consolation. Oh yes, and ya may be interested to hear that Birk is out of the hospital. His doctor said that if ya hadn't airlifted him off the Washington Monument when ya did, then he might not have survived. Luckily, all he came down with is a touch of fukkin pneumonia."

"You know I only allowed that shitbrained nutsack to come down after his fuknugget of a wife started to assbadger me," retorted Crump, while clicking his fingers to request another diet coke. "I didn't even know the fukker was married until the other week. Of course, I'd seen her around but always assumed she was one of the hookers that Mylo hangs out with when his wife is back in Mississippi with their 11 kids. Now, Bich, are you going to give me a progress report on the fukkin East Wing or just sit there on your ass spouting shit?"

"I was fixin' to, Mr. President," acknowledged Bich, with a broad grin. "It was a brilliant idea of ya's to award a Crump dummy company the contract to rebuild the East Wing and then get undocumented immigrants to do all the fukkin work. We're payin' them a dollar an hour and then chargin' the goddamn taxpayer millions."

"Bich, don't forget those shittossers have to pay for their own meals, and obviously that's always catered by Crumpburger. By the time the job is finished, they won't have earned so much as a dicksneeze of a dime," laughed Crump, as I conscientiously noted everything down in my notepad. "And, Trenton, here's the kicker, we're charging them for lodging on the South Lawn of the Crump House. It's really an old circus tent that we picked up for practically nothing, but we still bill the taxpayer $100 a night for every one of the fukkers. Needless to say, they have to sleep on the bare ground, but it's not like we're in the middle of winter, it's halfway through January already."

"Mr. President, I believe the repairs will be completed by the middle of next month. We can then have ICE arrest the fukkers and ship them back to whatever shithole country they came from," reported Bich, while flicking through her notes. "The only other thing ya should be aware of is that Twatt Jabowsky has managed to get you an endorsement from Rusty Beaver."

"And who the fukwag is Rusty Beaver when he's at home?" thundered Crump, as he eyeballed the First Lady sliding down the stairway handrail of Air Force One. "Sounds like a real assbender if you ask me."

"He's the fukkin teen singin' sensation from Canada with a dozen number one hits under his belt. And by all accounts he's an aspirin' Crumper once he gets his citizenship papers approved," explained Bich, who was secretly one of his biggest admirers. "It sure is a pity that his fans, the Beaverettes, are mostly young gals below the age of 15. After Rusty's endorsement, I reckon they'd have been a sure bet to vote for ya, Mr. President."

"Then issue each of them a shitass fake ID and register the fukkers as Republicans so that they can vote by mail. Shifty Daniels can help. He'll know plenty of people in the slammer who could do a job like this," directed Crump, who happened to be the Republican Party's principal proponent of mail-in voter fraud."

The following afternoon I was sitting in the Oval Office and shooting the breeze with Crump when a staffer walked in to announce the arrival of another top Crump campaign donor. Dic Hade was the president of the powerful gun lobby, the American Society of Shooters, or ASS as it was most commonly known. Notably, his organization was made up of over 25 million ASS men, but only three women, one of whom was Bich Landers. Not surprisingly, they were all diehard Crumpers and gun-toting vigilantes to the core. And each of them had the misguided belief that the Second Amendment gave them the right to arm themselves with just about every gun known to man.

Although ASS called itself America's largest civil rights organization, I felt a touch of irony that their members did not believe in the rights of others. Namely, to not get shot by a heavily armed crazed fukker with a gun. Seeing as I came from a country where gun ownership was mostly banned, and shootings were few and far between, I was very much looking forward to meeting such a prominent ASS man. And once I saw the six-foot-six Dic Hade with an AR-15 and high-capacity 100-round magazine slung over one of his shoulders, I was not disappointed in the least.

"Crump, you old cocksucker, how are you doing?" roared Dic, who certainly stood out in the suit and tie wearing Crump House with his military-style camouflaged body armor and candy apple red ASS cap. "I've been telling you for years to carry a fukkin handgun. If you had taken my advice, you could have capped that Fudrucker supporter who attacked you the other month. You know the one who was all over SHITE news for weeks but the fake press claimed it was nothing more than a false alarm caused by your press secretary."

"I may not carry a gun, Dic, but as you know, I've always been an ASS man at heart," replied Crump, as Dic Hade laid his rifle down on the resolute desk. Then along with his two backup magazines, a pair of Glock 9mms, and half a dozen flash-bang grenades, he placed a long molded black plastic carrying case on the desk as well. "Dic, you look like you're about to start a goddamn fukkin war."

"You better believe it, Mr. President. We've got one too many fukstruck pussyfooting liberals in this country, and that means war is inevitable," proclaimed Dic, while patting his AR-15 and grinning. "But no fear, me and my fellow ASS men are ready to purge this country of all those shitdick never-Crumper fukkers at a moment's notice."

"Dic, it's good to hear that I have an ASS man of your renown behind me and 25 million more patriotic ASS men standing in line to take your place," declared Crump, as he slapped Dic Hade on the back. "Now, before we start, I need to introduce you to my presidential intern, Trenton Begby. And by the way, Trenton here is from England."

"England. I tried setting up an ASS country office in England about five years ago. It ended up being a total and utter fukfest for us. ASS was there for two years before we realized there were only seven guns on the whole shitass island, and five of those were rusty relics manufactured during the First World War. Not even your boys in blue carry guns. All they're allowed to do over there is throw their jagoff helmets and dickslap you with a goddamn baton," exclaimed Dic, who was shaking his head in dismay. "What sort of democracy is that when you can't shoot up the neighborhood when you feel like it? In this great country of ours, we've absolutely no idea how many fukkin guns there are or for that matter who has them. And mark my words, ASS, under my continued leadership, is determined to keep it that way."

"But I read somewhere that gun crime and mass shootings are out of control in the United States, and they're increasing exponentially every year," I stated, a little defensively. "I have it written here in my notepad that half a million people were shot during the past 12 months, and there were nearly 200,000 fatalities. Don't you think that if the country enacted some form of gun control, then shootings would decline, and many American lives could be saved?"

"Trenton, the fukkers in the fake press always like to blow everything out of proportion. In actual fact, the number of shootings in this country is no more than comparable nations like Afghanistan, Yemen, and Syria," retorted Dic, while crushing an empty diet coke can against his forehead. "What you fail to understand is that guns need bullets, and so every shot fired means money in the pockets of ammunition manufacturers. Along with the firearms manufacturers, they pay ASS a shitload of cash, and the more guns and ammo they sell, the more greenbacks come my way. What I'm most proud of during my tenure at ASS is that we have increased mass shootings by over 50% year over year. And you may not be aware of this, but every time the fake press report another mass shooting, then gun and ammo sales fukkin skyrocket. The shooting business has never been better, although my fellow ASS men and I, with the help of the President, plan to double shootings within the next three years."

"My base is predominantly comprised of ASS men, Trenton. If it had not been for Dic Hade's ASS, I might never have been elected as president seven years ago," interjected Crump, as he leaned back on his chair. "Now, Dic, I hear that Smilin' Mo Fudrucker and LSD are running on gun control this election. If this is true, then what does ASS plan to do about it?"

"The goddamn Democrats are not only talking of gun control for adults, but the dickfuks want to keep guns out of the hands of kids as well," roared Dic, who nearly fell off his chair laughing. "I say let the assclowns talk all the shit they want. If they keep it up, then an ASS man is bound to step up and plug a few of those fukkin cockburgers. Mr. President, you've already decreed that the Second Amendment is the only part of the Constitution that stands. That means everyone, no matter how psychotic or demented they happen to be or however young they are, can arm themselves to the teeth. Not only that, they have the right to kill any fukker that so much as gives them a sideways glance. You know that from the moment I held my first gun at the age of six weeks, I knew I was going to be an ASS man. I never joined the military, but I've been shot 12 times during my life, and three of those bullets hit me square in the head. It never did me any real harm, and as an ASS man, I've always believed in my God-given right to stand my ground."

"Is that why you gunned down your fukkin mailman the other week?" chuckled Crump, while opening a can of diet coke and winking at me.

"I've told those fukwits at the USPS time and time again that they need to keep their hands where I can see them and wave a white flag when entering my property. How am I expected to tell a friend from an assjacking foe? My mantra is to shoot the fukker and then ask all the shitschmuck questions you want after," answered Dic, who was grinning and patting one of his Glocks as he spoke. "The fukheads at the Postal Service are griping about losing 16 mailmen at my address over the past 10 years. I say who gives a fuk, they're ten a penny and probably assmunching never-Crumpers anyway."

"Dic, whatever happened to that new type of gun you were going to try out? You know, the one with the smart technology that the assheads in Congress were so excited about. I believe it had some sort of chip in the trigger that could detect whether you're a crazy fukker and if so, it wouldn't fire," asked Crump, as he emptied his can of diet coke.

"Oh, you mean that useless piece of shit the Democrats were pushing. Whoever the fukwizard was who came up with that assbrained idea deserves a bullet through the fukkin head," fumed Dic, as he unwisely pressed one of the Glocks to his own head to emphasize the point. "ASS received a consignment of them last month, and they were all duds. I personally tested every gun, and not one of them fired. It was the same with every ASS man who pulled the trigger. Of course, that dickrattler, LSD, got her hands on them and fired each one live on DNN. What that was meant to demonstrate escapes me, but the fukkers in the fake press made a kissass big deal about it all the same."

"Fukkers, all of them," blurted Crump, who was shaking his

41

head as he grasped hold of Dic Hade's Glock and passed it to me for safekeeping. "Dic, you made a point of saying business is good and that ASS is making a killing. What I want to know is how you're going to send more of it my way. As you know, if you scratch my back, then I'll be happy to scratch your ASS."

"I'm glad you brought that up, Mr. President. We had a shitstorming session at ASS only the other week, and the boys and I came up with three fukkin awesome ideas," reassured Dic, with a smile on his face. He then pulled something that resembled a candy apple red credit card from one of the pockets in his body armor and handed it to Crump. "We're calling it the ASSCARD, and it's like a credit card but offers so much more. The fukkers pay $99 a year, and instead of cashback or shitster points, they get free ammo. The numbers guys at ASS are thinking of a bullet for every $10 spent. Every ASSCARD holder automatically becomes a member of ASS, if they're not one already, and they also receive a 5% discount at Crumpburger. If you can have your associates at Crumpburger push the card to every customer that comes by, then we're sure going to make a fukload of cash."

"Interesting, Dic, but offering discounts to just any old fukker is not the Crump way," contended Crump, as I jotted down his words in my notepad. "What precisely am I going to get out of this fukkin deal?"

"Don't worry about the discount, Mr. President. Crump-burger sales are bound to soar, so you'll make your money back on volume. And the jackasses will never read the small print on the agreement. It states that if they don't pay off the full amount on their ASSCARD every 30 days, then we charge 100% interest per month," sniggered Dic, who was lighting a cigar as he leaned back on his chair. "Trust me, we'll fleece the dumbass fukkers, and your piece of the action is 25% of the annual fee and interest charges."

"Make it 50%, and you have yourself a deal," countered Crump, while giving me a wink.

"40% is all I can go, Mr. President, and you can open a Crumpburger at ASS headquarters in Wyoming," responded Dic, with one hand in the air and his palm facing Crump.

"Done, you sly fukker," agreed Crump, as he spat on his hand and gave Dic Hade a high five. "Now, what else do you have in mind?"

"Little Fukkers, Mr. President," grinned Dic, while puffing on his cigar.

"What about them?" probed Crump, who was eager to find out what the ASS man sitting before him was proposing."

"They were a ballsy fukass of an inspired idea, Mr. President. And it just happens that kids are on ASS's radar right now," confided Dic, as he carelessly dropped cigar ash on the Resolute desk. "ASS has a mission to arm every kid in the country, and Little Fukkers could make it a hell of a lot easier for us to achieve this. We'd like Crumpburger to give away a handgun with something like a dozen rounds of ammo for every 10 Little Fukkers purchased. Nothing fancy, just a cheap piece of shit will do. Once they get the feel of a real gun in their hands and bang off a few rounds, then they'll be assbadgering their fukkin parents to buy them more ammo and better guns when Christmas and birthdays come around."

"And so what's in it for me, Dic?" demanded Crump, who was leaning forward on his chair. "Last time I heard, guns cost money."

"Mr. President, here's the deal," revealed Dic, while blowing smoke rings into the air. "ASS can bring the guns and ammo in from North Korea. I'd tell you how much they'll cost us, but you'd probably piss your pants laughing. All I'm prepared to say is that we currently operate a firearms manufacturing facility near Pyongyang, where the Kims supply us with a crapload of forced labor. In exchange, we've been furnishing them with nuclear weapons technology given to us by one of your friends in the Russian government. We can run the guns by way of Cuba to avoid any awkward questions from the Feds. As I'm sure you're aware, the Castros operate most of the Crumpburger franchises in the Caribbean, so if you're on board, the fukkers will be happy to oblige us. From there, we can smuggle each consignment to our ASS compound in Alabama. ASS will pay for the guns and ammo, and naturally, we'll stamp everything with made in the US of A. All you have to do is handle distribution through your Crumpburger outlets. This will undoubtedly jack up sales of Little Fukkers, and that means more cash for you. And one more thing, Mr. President, we'll also give Crumpburger a fake invoice so that you can claim a fukkin tax deduction for the guns and ammo you give away."

"Dic, I like your style. You've got yourself a goddamn deal," affirmed Crump, as he spat on his hand once again and gave Dic Hade another high five. "So what's this other proposal you want to put forward? It's already getting late, so you better lay it on me before we run out of time. You know that only fukkin losers and assholes work after five."

"Well, I've been saving the best for last," Mr. President, smiled Dic, who put out the remains of his cigar before getting to his feet. Then he unlocked the carrying case he had brought with him and pulled out the intimidating-looking weapon that lay inside. "This bad boy is a military issue M4 Carbine Commando machine gun with a built-in grenade launcher and

300-round magazine, or at least it looks like one. ASS can get these copies from China at a quarter of the price of the genuine article, and they come with papers of authenticity stating that each one is manufactured right here."

"Whoa, Dic. You better be careful with that badass fukker, or you're liable to take out half the Oval Office, and me and Trenton with it," cautioned Crump, as he warily looked down the barrel of Dic Hade's machine gun.

"No need to sweat, Mr. President, the safety is on. Only a total fukwit would take the safety off when they are inside," laughed Dic, while returning the machine gun to its carrying case and placing it on the floor beside the Resolute desk. "As you're already aware, ASS believes the Second Amendment gives us the right to own any fukkin gun we want, and that includes machine guns. For that reason, I request you issue a decree giving ASS men the right to own and openly carry machine guns from now until the end of time."

"If ASS can make it worthwhile for yours truly, then I'll decree anything you fukkin ASS men want," imparted Crump, as he smiled and winked at me once again.

"Mr. President, ASS has got 25 million members who will pawn their bitchass mothers to buy an M4 Carbine Commando at a 25% discount. We won't tell the fukkers that they're Chinese copies, and ASS will cut you in for 50% of the profits," assured Dic, who had a grin like a Cheshire cat. "Our marketing boys have already come up with a new ad campaign that I think you'll like - The best way to stop a bad man with a gun is an ASS man with a machine gun. It's got a shitfukking ring to it, don't you think. And the kicker is that not only will ASS membership soar, but machine guns use a fukload of ammo, so the ammunition manufacturers will be over the moon. We forecast shootings will increase fivefold in the first year, and that means even regular people will be buying more fukkin guns. Except for the dickwad losers who are so shitbrained that they get themselves shot and carted off in the fukwagon, it's going to be a win-win deal all-round."

"Dic, I'll sign the goddamn decree right now and have Bich Landers set up a press briefing at the Crump House. And I will announce to the fukkers in the fake press that it goes into effect immediately," asserted Crump, with yet another saliva-laden high five that nearly knocked Dic Hade off his chair.

"Thank you, Mr. President. You won't regret this. As always, it's a privilege to do business with the Crump House," beamed Dic, who handed me an ASS cap and then placed two more on the Resolute desk beside Crump. "I'll have the contracts sent over to Sing Sing so that Shifty Daniels can give them the once-over. By the way, the spare ASS cap is for Jr. You must be proud of him; he sent at least a dozen fukkers to the cemetery last year to become one of our top-performing ASS men. It's a pity Birk never became an ASS man as well. That boy has got everything ASS looks for in a prospective member – dumb as fuk and access to a heap of cash."

It took several minutes for Dic Hade to gather up the weapons he had placed on the Resolute desk earlier that afternoon, and then I handed him the Glock I was still holding. As Crump scribbled a few words on a piece of Crumpburger embossed paper, I excitedly pulled out my phone to take a picture of the history-making moment. Then clutching his AR-15 in both hands, the president of ASS stood by Crump's side for the decree to be signed just as I called out, Say CHEESE, and snapped the photo that Crump would later tweet to his 100 million followers.

"Trenton, this is what the presidency is all about. I've made three deals this afternoon that are going to make me an assload of cash. Most of the fukbrained losers who came before me were simply amateurs. Although they were a corrupt bunch of mothafukkers that pretty much did as they pleased, only a handful of them understood the Founding Fathers created the presidency as an asscracking quasi-monarchy. You know, I'm the first president to acknowledge that I'm really the King of the United States and can do anything I fukkin want. And if you haven't done so already, you should jot that down in your notepad," declared the King (I mean, Crump), who was leaning back on his chair and laughing now that Dic Hade had left the Oval Office. "Fukkers with guns, don't you just love them."

"Crump, since I started my internship, I don't believe that I have ever seen you carry a gun," I asked, inquisitively. "As a matter of fact, you are one of the few people at the Crump House that doesn't walk around with a lethal weapon protruding from some part of their clothing. I'm used to it now, though before it was a little disconcerting seeing so many guns, especially when they seem to go off at inopportune moments throughout the day. Thank goodness the Crump House has a medical trauma team on call 24/7."

"Only crazy fukkers carry guns, Trenton, and there are enough of those working here. Trust me, guns are not for the likes of you and me. They're reserved for dumbfuks like Dic Hade and the rest of his fukkin ASS men. If it was not for the fact that those nutjobs are all loyal Crumpers and eat so many Crumpburgers, I'd lock up every one of the fukkers," maintained Crump, as he called Bich Landers on his phone, only to listen to it ring six times and go to voicemail. "The fukker is never around when I need her. Trenton, can you walk over to the press office, and if you find Bich, tell the cumbubble to get her ass over to the Oval Office right away. And bring OnYurway as well. Dic Hade has left that goddamn machine gun of his on the floor. Tell her I don't want to be tripping over the fukkin thing every time I go for a wazz, and that reminds me, nature calls, so I'll go for one while you're away."

As I was eager to please my gifted mentor, without delay, I jumped from my seat and marched down the corridor that led to the Crump House press office. Luckily, it did not take me any time at all to locate the press secretary because she was right where I expected her to be. Striding into her office, I could see Bich Landers sitting at a desk with a pair of headphones on and leaning back on a high-backed leather swivel chair. As was Bich's habit, her knee-high calfskin cowboy boots were resting on the head of a grizzly bear that she had shot and stuffed the previous winter. And she was leisurely delving into a pot of her prized redneck caviar using only her right index finger and drinking from a bottle of Arkansas root beer.

After I explained to her that she and OnYurway were summoned to the Oval Office, and they were to go posthaste, Bich licked her finger and said, "Righty-oh." She then accompanied me to the spartan-looking office that adjoined her own and called out to Crump's senior counselor. Oleander OnYurway was cleaning her magnums as we walked in, but once she had the nod from Bich, she reloaded her guns, and then we were on our way. Two minutes later, the three of us were entering the Oval Office, only to hear Crump turn the air blue as he circled the Resolute desk peering at the floor.

"Un-fukkin-believable! This is supposed to be the most secure and heavily guarded building on the planet. And what happens? Some thieving fukker waltzes right in here while I'm having a wazz and takes whatever they goddamn want," bellowed Crump, as he sat down on his chair and opened a can of diet coke. "I was only in the bathroom for five minutes, and when I returned, the assbagger had swiped one of those ASS caps and Dic Hades case with his shitfukker of a machine gun. So not only do we have a thieving fukker roaming the Crump House, but a thieving fukker with a fukkin big machine gun."

"I reckon it'll turn up sooner or later, Mr. President," grinned Bich, just as the Crump House sirens sounded for the first time since the incident in the Roosevelt Room.

It was at that moment I heard the sound of real machine gun fire for the first time in my life, and then all hell broke loose. With their guns drawn, two Secret Service agents burst into the Oval Office and screamed at Crump to hit the dirt. OnYurway pulled out her magnums, then before Crump knew what was happening, Bich dived on him. Knocking him off his chair, Crump landed on the wooden floor with a resounding thud, while the Crump House press secretary clung to him for dear life.

"Bich, if you don't get your sorry ass the fuk off me in the next three seconds, then I'll have OnYurway shoot you in the fukkin head," yelled Crump, who was giving Bich the fukeye and was looking about as hacked off as I had ever seen him. "And you two dicksticks who are supposed to be safeguarding me, the fukker with the machine gun is out there, not in here. If I see you fukups in the Oval Office again, then OnYurway will happily plug the both of you as well."

Once the Secret Service agents had left to reinforce a makeshift barricade that had been erected outside the door to the Oval Office, Bich helped Crump to his feet. Hearing the gunfire grow louder as the fukker with the machine gun moved closer, the four of us took cover behind the sturdy Resolute desk.

Then after a momentary silence in which I mistakenly thought our ordeal was finally over, the sound of a rocket-propelled grenade could be heard.

As it blew the barricade to smithereens along with most of the Oval Office door, a familiar voice was then heard by all. "I'm an ASS man, I'm an ASS man, and I'm going to the Moon," called out Birk, who was wearing an ASS cap and riding his tricycle up and down the main corridor of the West Wing. And resting on the handlebars was Dic Hade's military issue M4 Carbine Commando machine gun with its built-in grenade launcher and 300-round magazine. Though thankfully for everyone in the Crump House, Crump's youngest son had at long last run out of ammunition.

4

CRUMP on the Press

"Never listen to the fukkers in the fake press. Watch SHITE news instead!"
— Ronald S. Crump, President of the United States

* * *

"Howdy, Mr. President, and ya too, Trenton," called out Bich, as she glided into the Oval Office with Oleander OnYurway by her side. "I hope ya not going to get in a hissy fit again and cuss me out like yesterday. And don't forget that we have the press briefin' to announce ya machine gun decree at three. There's sure to be a shitload of the fake press attendin', so be prepared for some fukkin shitbrained questions."

Considering the West Wing had resembled a war zone only the day before, Crump had been in a remarkably good mood when I entered the Oval Office around noon. And even more surprising to me was that not only had the door to his office been replaced, there was also no sign of the gun battle that had taken place in the corridor. During our lunch in which we dined on Crumpburgers and diet coke, I learned that his legion of undocumented immigrants had labored through the night to complete the work. And even though it had cost him next to nothing, Crump bragged he had already invoiced the assheads in the US Treasury to the tune of a cool million for the whole fukkin job.

"So what else do you have for me, Bich?" asked Crump, who was leaning back on his chair and drinking from a can of diet coke.

"Mr. President, I've just received the incident report from yesterday's little mishap. I'm cock-a-hoop to inform ya that it's not as bad as we originally thought. There were only 14 casualties, five of which were fatal, and the other nine had non-life-threatenin' injuries. All of them were Secret Service agents, so no loss there, except for one of the deceased, who happened to be ya personal assistant. She was only a temp and by all accounts about as useless as fukkin tits on a bull. So Birk probably did us a favor by not havin' to shitcan her," shared Bich, as she turned the page of her Crump House press diary. "I've also spoken to the hospital, and they've already discharged Birk. According to the doctors, when ya told OnYurway to shoot him in the head, fortunately, the bullet went right through his brain and missed all of his vital organs. So he's right as rain, and ya gonna be pleased to hear that the mischievous little tyke is back in the Crump House ridin' his tricycle again."

"Well, that's just assfukkin great," snapped Crump, who picked up a Crumpburger and then threw it at OnYurway. "Trenton, if you want a fukkin job done right, then you always need to do it yourself. When Asyphilis, Tribianka, and I were vacationing with the Kims in North Korea last summer, I found out that they regularly deal with their unwanted fukkers themselves, and that includes family members. As a matter of fact, they blow them to kingdom come using an anti-aircraft gun. And they don't have someone else do it; the head honcho lines them all up in a field and fires the fukstick himself. I don't mind telling you that even Tribianka and I had a go. It was a real hoot and so much better than paying for fukkers to sit on their asses behind bars or wait years for a goddamn lethal injection. That reminds me, Bich, I want you to contact the General to have the US Army install an anti-aircraft gun in the Rose Garden so that I can dispense justice when I feel like it. And tell him to have the Army Corps of Engineers erect plenty of stadium seating for spectators. I can probably charge at least $1,000 a head, and with the number of fukkers I intend to send to the next world, it's going to make me a crapload of cash."

"Sure will do, Mr. President," nodded Bich, as she made a note of Crump's latest request. "Ya also goin' to be speakin' at another re-election rally tomorrow afternoon, and it's scheduled to take place in West Virginia. This one's sponsored by SHITE news, so the SHITE buddies will be joinin' ya on stage."

"West fukkin Virginia! Isn't that the one I nicknamed the Fuktard State because it's full of gun-toting nutjobs and goddamn assholes?" commented Crump, with an eye roll and a yawn.

"That's right, Mr. President, but most of the fukkers of votin' age in the state are Crumpers, and there's a Crumpburger on just about every street corner," pointed out Bich, rather enthusiastically.

"Bich, just make sure that you tell Twatt Jabowsky I expect a bigger crowd this time. And that doesn't mean he packs the stadium with their fukkin farm animals. You know I still remember the last rally we had in West Virginia. The goddamn hogs outnumbered the fukheaded people," hissed Crump, while pointing his right index finger at his press secretary as he browbeat her. "If he has to, Twatt should call up the local detention centers and fill the place with undocumented immigrants. No one will ever know, and tell the pisshead to instruct the Secret Service to shoot any of those shitbaggers that refuses to cheer and clap their hands when I'm on stage. Then after the rally is over, he can have the lot of them carted off and deported so that they don't get the opportunity to speak with any of those fukkers in the fake press."

"Alrighty," confirmed Bich, who was nonchalantly checking the time on her wristwatch. "Well butter my butt and call me a biscuit. How time flies, we better leave now, or we'll be late for our own briefin'. But before we go, Mr. President, your final engagement of the day will be a meetin' at four with Sergey Murdocov from SHITE news."

After a bout of bellyaching from Crump in which he claimed Bich was working him to the bone, the four of us marched out of the Oval Office. The Ronald S. Crump Press Briefing Room was conveniently located in the West Wing and therefore took us no time at all to walk there. Without hesitating, Bich and OnYurway opened the door and strode in, while Crump grabbed my arm and whispered in my ear that I should hang back for a moment. Then with a snigger, he pulled out a sharpie from his jacket pocket and crossed out the word, Press, on the nameplate attached to the door. Scrawling an entirely different word to replace it, Crump and I cracked up laughing before entering the now renamed, Fukkers Briefing Room.

Once inside, I could see a motley assemblage of people that

must have numbered around 50. Some were already seated while others were standing, and a few at the rear had shoulder-mounted cameras. All of them were chattering incessantly, so Bich yelled, "Fukkers, y'all need to shut ya goddamn yappin' for the President of the United States, Ronald S. Crump." Although a few turned to look at the Crump House press secretary, most simply continued their conversations until OnYurway pulled out her magnums and fired several shots into the air.

With the unruly members of the press now silent and sitting in their assigned seats with notepads and pens in hand, Crump stepped forward. Holding the decree, he stood at the podium sporting the newly reimagined Great Seal of the United States, in which was written, Crump Knows Best. Then in typical Crump fashion, he raised the decree above his head for all to see and declared machine guns were now legal for ASS men. And this, he recited with the aid of his notes, was because the best way to stop a bad man with a gun is an ASS man with a machine gun.

"Mr. President," called out Raz Alvarez of DNN, who was sitting in the front row of the briefing room with one arm in a sling and the other raised high in the air. "With the number of people shot in this country rising every year, don't you think that allowing those crackpot ASS men to carry machine guns is downright irresponsible?"

"Raz, are you fukkin deaf as well as dumb. I just said that the best way to stop a bad man with a gun is an ASS man with a machine gun. Do you and your shitwitted Democrat friends really want bad men to outgun our brave ASS men?" barked Crump, as he slammed his fist down on the podium while giving Raz the fukeye. "Who gives a shit if a few more fukkers get plugged here and there? Not me, and certainly not the patriotic

Crump-supporting citizens of this country."

"But according to your own Bureau of Alcohol, Tobacco, Firearms and Explosives, there's a direct correlation between gun sales and shootings. In fact, for every 10% increase in gun sales to the general population, the Bureau claims that shootings rise by 9.99%. And if you look at the numbers for ASS men, then shootings literally go off the scale," retorted Raz, before receiving a round of applause from her colleagues in the fake press.

"Fake news! Ya already on ya last goddamn warnin', Raz. So now I'm barrin' ya from askin' any more fukkin questions for a month. Go sit ya ass at the back of the room," interrupted Bich, as she signaled to OnYurway to escort Raz Alvarez to her new seat in the aptly named misbehaving fukkers section.

"Crump, what do you have to say about the shootings that took place yesterday in the Crump House?" yelled Loudmouth Lonnie Laverty from SBC, the outspoken associate of the popular SBC anchor, Stoner McCall. Who was still on suspension from the Crump House press corps over his fake news story regarding Tribianka and the Little Rock Hyenas. "My source in the Crump House said that a crazed ASS man shot up the West Wing with a machine gun and took out a dozen or so Secret Service agents. That hardly bodes well for your machine gun decree. Don't you agree?"

"Loudmouth, are ya bitchassin me again?" snarled Bich, as she sprang to her feet and stabbed the SBC reporter with an Arkansas toothpick that was strapped to her thigh. Then the Crump House press secretary called to OnYurway to drag Loudmouth Lonnie Laverty kicking and screaming from the room. "Sorry about that, Mr. President. It can get a bit rough in these briefin's, but at least the fukbag will think twice before mouthin' that kind of shit in ya presence in future."

"SHITE news has it on good authority a shotgun-wielding Fudrucker supporter was behind the ruckus in the Crump House yesterday afternoon," announced Vaj Ingersol from the SHITE buddies, once Bich had called for silence after the removal of the disruptive reporter. "If it had not been for the courageous actions of our quick-thinking President, more Secret Service agents would have lost their lives. Holding a machine gun in one hand, he heroically took out the armed assailant, so as a Crump-supporting Republican, I back this decree to the hilt. Now that every ASS man in the country can carry a machine gun to protect decent god-fearing Americans, this great nation of ours is going to be a much safer place to live."

"Bullcrap," muttered Jem Tossa from the National Broadcasting Service, albeit under his breath. Although fortunately for him, the Crump House press secretary was not entirely sure which of the reporters sitting in the briefing room it had been. However, she did have her suspicions.

"Tossa, for your sake, I hope that wasn't you," warned Bich, as she pointed the blade of her bloodstained Arkansas toothpick directly at him.

"Of course not, Bich, you must be hearing things again," sniggered the NBS reporter, followed by a titter of laughter from some of the others in the room. "Mr. President, I do have a question that many NBS viewers around the country have been asking. ASS is currently being investigated by federal and state authorities for suspected money laundering, gun running, receiving bribes from foreign governments, bribing US government officials, fraud, and tax evasion. You've closely aligned yourself with ASS over the years and appear to have quite a cozy relationship with its president. So what I would like to know is just how far into Dic Hade's ASS are you?"

"I can assure you that the Crump administration has examined Dic Hade's ASS thoroughly. And we have always found it to be as clean as a fukkin whistle," replied Crump, who was waving his hand at his irate press secretary to stand down. "If you fukkers in the fake press want to spread shitass dispersions about a fine organization like ASS, then you better be prepared for an ASS man with a machine gun to give you a bona fide fukover."

"Right, that's enough from you, Tossa," cautioned Bich, as Crump took a seat next to me, and then the Crump House press secretary stepped forward to take her place at the podium. "Now, y'all listen up, on behalf of the Crump administration, I would like to offer my condolences to one of our own who died by suicide yesterday. Although Chester Ligget of the New York Whimper was a shitbreathin' lameass fukker, he was a member of the Crump House press corps and doubtlessly will be missed by someone. I'm sure that his timely passin' will be forgotten soon enough, but in the meantime, we'll have three seconds of silence for Chester."

"Suicide! He was found in his apartment with his hands bound behind his back. And not only that, he'd been shot twice in the back of the head with bullets from a .44 magnum," shouted out Jem Tossa, as he pointed his finger at Bich. "And I find it more than a bit of a coincidence that he died only hours after the press briefing in which you called him, and I quote, An asslickin' Democratic shitbag, followed by, Ya a walking coffin, Ligget.

"That was just a bit of friendly professional banter," raged Bich, while pulling out her Arkansas toothpick once again and plunging it into the top of the wooden podium. "And it's fake news that he was shot two times in the back of the head. It was actually three, and that was because fukkin Chester was such a godawful bad shot. The President's senior counselor, Oleander OnYurway, personally led the investigation, so if ya call it anything but suicide, ya can step outside and toss the shit with her."

After Jem Tossa turned around to see OnYurway fingering her magnums and smiling, as she often liked to do, he quietly returned to his seat. And for the rest of the briefing, the NBS reporter wisely maintained a low profile by keeping his big mouth shut. Once the three seconds of silence was over, during which Crump muttered the words, "Total fukker," Chester Ligget's name was never brought up again. Then with several hands raised in the air, Bich selected a reporter from Citizens Public Radio to ask the next dumbass question.

"Mr. President, you have nominated yourself for the Nobel Peace Prize for each year of your presidency and have lost every time. Do you believe this year will be any different?" asked Mallory Hightower of CPR, an octogenarian of 60 years standing in the press corps.

"I could nuke every fukker on the planet if I felt like it, but I choose not to. If that's not worthy of the Nobel Peace Prize, then I don't know what is," grumbled Crump, as he rolled his eyes in resentment at the irksome CPR reporter. "Those goddamn cockbites in Oslo better pick the right nominee this year, and if they don't know already, that's Crump. If not, I just might nuke the fukkin lot of them in Greenland and have done with it."

"Mr. President, Mr. President, Mr. President," hollered the high-strung Dillard Wowser from the Washington Ghost, who had his hand up, and as usual, was getting himself into a tizzy. "There have been reports that your CRAPs are unsafe, and conditions for the elderly residents living in them are often intolerable. How do you respond to these accusations? And what would you like to say to the readers of the Washington Ghost to reassure them their aging relatives are well cared for in Crump Retirement Palaces?"

"Listen, Wowser, nobody loves an old fukker more than Crump. My own beloved mother is an old fukker, and I can tell you that she loves my CRAPs and wouldn't live anywhere else. Only the lying dickweasels from the fake press say otherwise. If you would like to take a closer look at one of my CRAPs, I'd be happy to oblige you," responded Crump, while giving OnYurway a Machiavellian style wink. "And let me tell you this once and for all, my CRAPs have an exemplary safety record. Only two of them have sunk since I first introduced the concept to our dear old fukkers. And though all hands were lost, no one really gives a shit, because let's face it, they would have kicked the fukkin bucket sooner or later anyway. Now, that's all the questions I'm going to answer for today, so I'll leave you fukkers in Bich and OnYurway's capable hands."

Crump gestured to me that it was time to leave, and though Bich and OnYurway remained in the briefing room, Vaj Ingersol returned with us to the Oval Office. Upon entering, we were greeted by the sight of a well-dressed elderly balding man with a rather pronounced squint. He was pulling up the zipper of his pants using his right hand while taking shots from a bottle of cheap Russian vodka he was holding in his left. And on her knees, but hurriedly getting to her feet, was Crump's most senior advisor and only daughter, Tribianka.

"Ah, Sergey, I see that you're getting the royal Crump House welcome," chuckled Crump, who shook hands with the elderly man before strolling over to the Resolute desk. "Trenton, this is Sergey Murdocov. Amongst other things, he's the chairman and owner of SHITE news. Sergey, this is my presidential intern, Trenton Begby. He's from England, and of course, you already know Vaj."

I was familiar with the name Sergey Murdocov as I had read about him on the SHITE news website and in numerous articles written by the fake press. He was a self-made billionaire from Russian with close ties to the Kremlin and the autocratic leader who had run the country for the past 30 years. In the 80s, he became a US citizen with the sole purpose of expanding his London-based media empire and making a killing in the land of opportunity. Although it should be noted, before his naturalization, he had never actually lived in his adopted country a day in his life. And interestingly, to this day, he still hasn't. SHITE news had been his brainchild after recognizing that what the American people really wanted in their lives was a fact-free conservative news network. So from his palatial home in London, gleefully, Murdocov gave it to them in the form of SHITE news.

"Crump, you goddamn double-dealing fukker, it's good to see you again. I've just flown in from London and will be heading back there this evening after I pay a visit to the nerve center of SHITE news. This country has made me a pile of cash, but I never like to spend more than a few hours here if I can help it. There are far too many whackos living in this crazy fukkin country for my liking. Especially the gun-toting kind like Dic Hade and his ASS men," thundered Murdocov, who took another shot of vodka and then offered the bottle to me. "That'll put hairs on your chest, Trenton. It's the secret to a long life - a couple of bottles of vodka a day and as many hookers as you feel like. Trust me; stick with that regimen, and you'll easily make it to a hundred."

"It's not often we get a visit from you, Sergey. So what brings you all the way across the pond to the Crump House?" inquired Crump, as he leaned back on his chair with Tribianka sitting on his lap.

"Campaign contributions, Crump," winked Murdocov, while unzipping a large roll bag full of cash that was sitting on the floor next to the sofa. "There's a $100 million here in 20s and 50s, and Vladimir said they look as good as the real thing thanks to the plates you gave him. You can have the lot for $10 million. That's my cut, and the rest is for you. Just make sure you veto every last one of those fukkin sanctions on Russia that the fukkers in Congress keep coming up with. And if there's anything SHITE news can do to boost you in the polls, then ask away. As you know, I don't give a shit about politics, but there is more money to be made with you and the Republicans in power than the dickwaving Democrats."

"Sounds good to me, Sergey," acknowledged Crump, as he helped himself to a can of diet coke. "I take it you'll be voting by mail again this election?"

"Of course, and unlike most of the lazy fukkers in this country, I paid good hard cash for my citizenship. That means I get to vote as many times as I goddamn like. Voter fraud is such a uniquely American thing, you've got to love it," laughed Murdocov, while emptying the last of the vodka. "Well, it's time to go. I can't waste my valuable time with idle fukkin chat when there's money to be made. Vaj, you're coming with me. It was a pleasure to meet you, Trenton. And Tribianka, I look forward to the same again next time."

The following day I boarded Air Force One with Crump for our short hop from Washington, DC to the lively city of Charleston, the capital of West Virginia. Along with the fake press from the Crump House press corps, most of whom I had met the previous afternoon, accompanying us were the SHITE buddies, Twatt Jabowsky, Bich Landers, Oleander OnYurway, Tribianka, and Waywerd Pushover. It was a treat for me that I got to ride with Crump and Tribianka in the presidential state car, or, the Beast, as it had been nicknamed, while the rest of our party rode behind us in a motorcade comprising 40 cars, a dozen Bradley Fighting Vehicles, and two M1 Abrams tanks.

As West Virginia had more than its fair share of ASS men, the Secret Service was not only armed to the teeth, but Crump wore a bulletproof vest under his suit, and coincidentally so did I. By the time we reached the stadium where the rally was to be held, he was already grumbling about the uncomfortable body armor. And not unexpectedly, Crump went to great lengths to complain about how much he hated this fukkin dicksneeze of a state. Then after he saw the size of the crowd that barely filled a quarter of the stadium, he muttered something uncomplimentary about Twatt Jabowsky before exiting the Beast.

This was my first Crump rally, and my initial impression was that it looked akin to a rowdy English football match. That is, aside from the fact the attendees all wore candy apple red ASS caps, had long bushy beards, and carried guns. Though the crowd lacked the numbers Crump yearned for, as there could not have been more than 10,000 Crumpers in attendance, their diminutive size was more than made up by their exuberance. Chanting, "Crump! Crump! Crump!" and firing their guns into the air as we entered the stadium, Crump waved at the crowd while making his way to an ornate golden chair that resembled a kingly throne.

"Who's your Daddy," shouted Crump, with his hands raised high.

"Crump is! Crump is! Crump is!" chanted every Crumper in the stadium, along with the SHITE buddies and the Crump House staff.

"I love West Virginia," yelled Crump, once he was standing on the stage. And then the crowd erupted into another round of chants for Crump before firing their guns into the air once again. "When I was growing up in New York, my dear old father used to take all us Crumps to West Virginia every summer. I still have fond memories of standing on the beach and looking out to sea, and that's why West Virginia is the only state for me."

Although, in reality, West Virginia is a landlocked state whose easternmost point is some 150 miles from the Atlantic Coast, that didn't stop the crowd throwing their ASS caps into the air as they called out Crump's name. Then taunting the Crumpers standing before him, Crump asked them what they wanted him to do with Smilin' Mo Fudrucker. Chanting, "Fuk him up! Fuk him up! Fuk him up!" the crowd went wild as Crump raised his arms once more before taking his rightful place on the throne.

What came next was a complete eye-opener for me because after the crowd went silent, Tribianka stepped forward with a microphone in hand and began to sing.

"CRUMP IS SIMPLY THE BEST
BETTER THAN ALL THE FUKKIN REST
WAY BETTER THAN FUDRUCKER
AND EVERY OTHER DEMOCRATIC FUKKER..."

After singing the first few verses solo, a catchy hip-swinging backing track from the 80s started up that could be heard throughout the stadium. Then Vaj Ingersol joined in along with Dicker Polson, Ranting Prick Enderbee, and the Crump House staff. At which point, I noticed the lyrics of the song were being projected onto giant screens so that the Crumpers could join in too. Needless to say, it was a sight to behold as the stadium reverberated with the booming sound of 10,000 tumultuous souls singing their hearts out. And of course, as a young Englishman, it was fascinating for me to experience American democracy up close. Then after fireworks were lit to light up the darkening afternoon sky in the colors of the flag, Crump stood up on stage to make his presidential campaign speech.

"Fuk Fudrucker! Fuk LSD and the rest of the Posse! And Fuk the Democrats!" yelled Crump, who was standing again with his fist in the air. And then he returned to the throne, where a giggling Tribianka joined him to sit on his lap.

"Fuk 'em up! Fuk 'em up! Fuk 'em up!" chanted the crowd, while firing their guns into the air yet again. Then an ASS cap wearing Bich Landers ran onto the stage with a 12 gauge pump-action shotgun she had concealed somewhere on her person and began to fire a few shots of her own.

"Ya-hoo!" cried out Bich, just as Crump gestured to OnYurway to restrain her as she was shooting precariously close to him. "This is just like a good ol' family gatherin' back home in Arkansas."

Once OnYurway had pistol-whipped the Crump House press secretary senseless and dragged her off the stage, Crump left Tribianka sitting on the throne as he stepped up to the podium. He then boasted that the size of the crowd in the stadium was the largest since time began and that Smilin' Mo Fudrucker would not have been able to muster a quarter of this number. Then over the next 90 minutes, Crump launched into a diatribe of reasons why every problem in the country was down to his presidential opponent and the fukkin Democrats.

Despite the fact that Crump had been the President for the past seven years and not Smilin' Mo Fudrucker, his profanity-laced rant went down a treat with every Crumper in the stadium. With the crowd cheering him on and repeatedly firing their guns into the air, Crump finished his speech by ridiculing his opponent and calling him an assbrained fukless wonder with no chance of winning. Crump then introduced the SHITE buddies onto the stage and passed the microphone to Ranting Prick Enderbee before returning to his seat on the throne and signaling to me to join him.

"I'm going to give myself a fukkin A+ for that speech," grinned Crump, as I proudly stood beside him. "Trenton, you should jot this down in your notepad. Never offer a solution to a problem. Instead, you should always look for someone to blame. In my opinion, scapegoats are invariably more useful than solutions."

By the time the SHITE buddies had finished denouncing Smilin' Mo Fudrucker as an assclown liberal and claiming the Democrats wanted to steal the election, Crump looked visibly bored. As he walked back to the podium, he noticed that Waywerd Pushover was making his way to one of the restrooms, some 50 feet from the stage. Jokingly, Crump called out to the crowd that Fudrucker was in the stadium and pointed at his chief of staff. It was at that point Crump's West Virginia re-election rally descended into what was described by one reporter as an out-and-out Crumper fukfest.

Only seconds after hearing the first volley of shots from several of the irate Crumpers, the Secret Service jumped into action by storming the stage to protect the President. Then while Waywerd Pushover hid in the closest restroom, Crump was carried off by half a dozen agents to the waiting Beast. Meanwhile, I grabbed Tribianka's hand and pulled her to safety at the same time as the Crump House staff and members of the press scurried for cover.

Pandemonium erupted as more and more Crumpers fired their guns in our general direction, only for the Secret Service to return fire in a vain attempt to protect us. Thinking that all was lost, I wrote a few words in my notepad for my parents, and then Tribianka and I tried to make our way to the motorcade. Before we could get even a quarter of the way there, I heard the roar of a diesel engine and the sound of tank tracks. And then, to my astonishment, an M1 Abrams tank came crashing through the stadium wall with its .50 caliber heavy machine gun blazing.

"I gotta get one of these for Granny," screamed Bich, who had obviously recovered from her pistol-whipping as she was the one driving the tank. Then pointing its main gun in the direction of the incoming gunfire, she fired an explosive round into the crowd before reloading the machine gun and chasing after the fleeing Crumpers.

5

CRUMP on the Military

"If you're a dumbfuk with a death wish, then the military is for you!"
— Ronald S. Crump, President of the United States

* * *

"Massacre!" screamed Crump, who I could see was flicking through the news channels while sitting on his chair at the Resolute desk when I walked into the Oval Office the following afternoon. And I couldn't help notice that he had been throwing Crumpburgers at the television again as there were tomato ketchup stains on the screen and burgers strewn all over the floor. "I'm the goddamn President of the United States, and so it's up to me to decide whether something is a fukkin massacre. Not those fukkers in the fake press. I've got a mind to have OnYurway get rid of the lot of them shitbaggers once and for all. And where's Bich? She's the jackass that got us into this clusterfuk of a mess in the first place by going asscrazy in that fukbanger of a tank."

After I switched the channel to SHITE news, almost immediately, Crump calmed down and opened a can of diet coke. The SHITE buddies were on, and Dicker Polson was interviewing Twatt Jabowsky and Skeeter Shiznit. Needless to say, they were discussing the Crump rally in West Virginia in which many of us, including myself, were lucky to escape unscathed. Unlike my recollection of the incident, Crump's campaign manager was shitwagging about an armed insurrection by Fudrucker supporters and undocumented immigrants. Then Crump's dirty trickster, who was not actually at the event, claimed he saw Smilin' Mo Fudrucker instigating the shoot-out in the stadium. And then Vaj Ingersol backed this up by insisting she heard Crump call out the Democratic Party presidential nominee's name.

Seeing Crump nod his head in agreement with the SHITE buddies and his campaign staff, I decided it was a good time to update him as to the last known whereabouts of the Crump House press secretary. Once the Secret Service had gotten Crump into the Beast the previous afternoon, they had wasted no time at all to get him to the safety of Air Force One. Then with droves of Crumpers running from the stadium and Bich in the M1 Abrams tank in hot pursuit, the rest of us, with the help of the Secret Service, had been able to make our escape. The only person in our party that was left behind was Waywerd Pushover, who was still cowering in the restroom when our motorcade headed back to the airport. As no one gave a shit about Crump's son-in-law, including his wife, that only left Bich. According to several members of the fake press, she was last seen driving the fully gassed tank towards the West Virginia – Kentucky border. And as of this morning, I had to inform Crump that she was still nowhere to be found.

"I can't say that I really give a fuk. There's no shortage of shitbrained asswipes in this place to take over the post of press secretary. Trenton, let's face it, any fukker could do that job," exclaimed Crump, as he handed me a can of diet coke. "Of course, I would have preferred for some of the fukkers in the fake press to have met their maker. Oh well, there's always next time."

As Crump laughed out loud while leaning back on his chair, I heard the rumbling of a diesel engine and the din of noisy tank tracks tearing up a tarmac surfaced road nearby. By the time Crump and I reached the Oval Office window and were peering out over the South Lawn, we could hear the sound of a wall being demolished and railings ripped from the ground. Then seconds later, an M1 Abrams tank came into view, and laying waste to the freshly mowed and painstakingly manicured lawn, it passed by our window. And that's when we saw the Crump House press secretary waving to us, and soon after that, a dozen Secret Service agents swarmed the tank with their guns drawn.

Following a call made to Oleander OnYurway, Crump and I had to wait a good 30 minutes for Bich Landers to be escorted into the Oval Office. Thankfully for her, not a single Secret Service agent had discharged their weapon when confronted by the intruder in the tank. And for the agents on duty, it was even more fortunate for them that the tank had run out of ammunition long before the press secretary arrived back at the Crump House.

"Howdy, Mr. President, and ya too, Trenton," called out Bich, as she and OnYurway entered the Oval Office. "Well, I declare that sure was a hoot of a fukkin party we had yesterday, but drivin' that darn tank all the way back here has plum worn me slap out."

"Bich, I've told you before, and I'll tell you again, you're a real shitmagnet. It was supposed to be a re-election rally and not an all-out fukathon. They may have been a worthless bunch of fukkers, but those ASS men were Crumpers. And more importantly to me, good-paying customers of Crumpburger," lectured Crump, while waving his arms in the air. "And what the fuk were you doing in that goddamn tank in the first place? I didn't even know you could fukkin drive."

"Ya know how I get when I'm all riled up, Mr. President. When I heard those fukkers start shootin', I had to come and save ya, and then I just got caught up in the moment," replied Bich, while grinning at Crump, who was giving her the fukeye. "And a tank is no different than a fukkin tractor, except for all the guns, of course. I've never passed a drivin' test in my life, but back home in Arkansas they teach all us young'uns to drive a tractor even before we're knee-high to a grizzly bear's ass. So drivin' that little ol' tank was about as natural to me as milkin' a goddamn possum."

Due to the fiasco in Charleston, Crump barred Bich Landers from attending any of his re-election rallies for a month. While his press secretary was in the proverbial fukhouse, Crump toured the country by making speeches in all of the 49 states except for Alaska, Hawaii, and needless to say, West Virginia. With the SHITE buddies shitwagging to their viewers each day and Skeeter Shiznit making up all kinds of shit about Smilin' Mo Fudrucker and LSD, Crump's ratings soared. And though this pleased him immensely, Crump told me that flying to so many shitass states full of fukbrained assbaggers just gave him one hell of a mindfuk.

By the time Good Friday came around, Crump was in a surprisingly amiable mood. No doubt because the US Army had installed his very own anti-aircraft gun in the Rose Garden. I was sitting with Crump in the Oval Office, and we were waiting for the chairman of the Joint Chiefs of Staff, General Merv Shizerstrom. He was the one who was going to instruct Crump on how to use the weapon, and I assumed, give him some sort of national security briefing. Though as Crump often reminded me, there was nothing the assheads in the military could tell him that he didn't know already. And besides, he received all the intel he ever needed by watching SHITE news.

It was not long after we had finished our lunch of Crump-burgers and played two games of Twister with Tribianka that Crump's new personal assistant called to say the General had arrived. Barely five minutes later, there was a firm knock on the door, and then a grey-haired man, who was somewhat short in stature and must have been in his 70s, walked into the Oval Office with his cap under one arm. He was dressed in a military uniform with five stars on his shoulders and a dozen or more medals pinned to the left breast of his jacket. And as he saluted Crump with his right hand, I could see that in his left, he carried what looked very much like an old beat-up toolbox with the Crumpburger logo printed on one side.

"Merv, you old fukker, I see that you're not dead yet," laughed Crump, as he shook the outstretched hand of the General. "Have you taken a look at the shitters in the Crump House yet? As you know, I like a shitter that's clean enough to eat off."

"Not yet, Mr. President. I parked my tank next to the Crumpburger drive-thru out front and then came straight here," answered the General, who was holding up the toolbox he had been carrying. "You've known me long enough to know that I never go anywhere without my trusty plunger and a bottle of industrial-strength bleach. I can give every last one of your shitters the Shizerstrom once-over after we've finished here."

"That's music to my ears, Merv. If the rest of the wretched fukkers in this place were as reliable as you, then I'd be king of the goddamn world and not just this dicksneeze of a country," affirmed Crump, as he returned to his chair at the Resolute desk. "Oh yes, and before I forget, this young man is Trenton Begby. He's my presidential intern from England, and I consider him my right-hand man. And of course, you've known Tribianka since she was ass-high to a fukkin midget."

"Ah, it's an honor to meet you, Sir," saluted the General, as I stood before him and grinned. And then Tribianka took her usual seat on Crump's lap as I sat on the sofa with General Merv Shizerstrom. "I hear that England is a fine place to live. I've never been north of New York City myself, but one day I intend to make it all the way up to Maine."

"Yes, it is, General," I replied, a little apprehensively. Although, I chose not to set the most senior commander in the United States military straight regarding the fact I was not actually from New England. Then thinking it was odd that a 5-star general carried a plunger, and even stranger that Crump had asked him to clean the Crump House toilets, I took a closer look at his collection of medals. Noticing the letter C was stamped on each one of them, I managed to muster up the courage to ask him a question. "General, before you became the chairman of the Joint Chiefs of Staff, which branch of the military did you serve in? Was it the US Army, Marine Corps, or Air Force?"

"None of them, Sir, I was never in the military. I started cleaning the shitters at Crumpburger once I reached my twelfth birthday. The President's father, God rest the crazy fukker's soul, gave me the job. And though he never paid me a penny for the first 25 years, I got to eat my fill of Crumpburgers every day and have never looked back," answered the General, who was proudly pointing to his medals as he spoke. "The President can tell you that I've earned every last one of these the hard way, in the trenches with my arms elbow-deep in all kinds of shit."

"That's all true. When it came to unblocking and cleaning the shitters, Merv was the best we ever had at Crumpburger. We called him the General because he always came through for us, no matter how much of a fukkin mess our shitster customers made. That's why after I sustained an injury during the Vietnam War and joined Crumpburger, I made him Vice President of Sanitation. All my employees do two years of shit duty now, including the goddamn managers, and Merv was the one who trained them. I call it Crump University, and believe me, it's the best business grounding anyone can get. The fukkers get covered from head to toe in shit, and then we have them flip burgers. Naturally, the dumbfuk customers never know, so who gives a crap," chuckled Crump, and so did Tribianka. "Trenton, an army marches on its shitters, which is how we won the war in Vietnam. That's why Merv was my top pick to command the military because I knew he would ensure the fukkers in uniform had the cleanest shitters of any armed forces in the world. Besides, the regular generals are all assmunching scrotelickers that have no idea what the fuk they're doing most of the time."

"Crump, I wasn't aware that you fought in Vietnam or had ever served in the military," I remarked, as I helped myself to a can of diet coke. "You've never mentioned it before, but I have heard that many war heroes don't like to talk about their ordeals and often keep what they went through to themselves."

"I didn't say that I was in the goddamn war. What I said was that I was injured during the Vietnam War," pointed out Crump, while reaching for a can of diet coke. "Trenton, only assholes join the military, and if there's a war going on, you've got to be a real fukhead to get yourself drafted. When the war in Vietnam was raging, it was tough on all of us, I can tell you. I had to hide out for a whole fukkin year in that hellhole called the Hamptons. It wasn't just champagne, partying, and high-priced hookers, you know. There were times when the boredom of war really set in, and all you could do to get yourself out of it was to snort two eight balls of coke and go on a fukkin spending spree. It took the fukbags from the draft board over a year to catch me, but I was diagnosed with an ingrown toenail by then. Or at least that's what my old man paid the doctor to write on my draft deferment so I could be declared unfit for duty."

"Mr. President, I remember that day well," chimed in the General, who was sitting bolt upright on the sofa with a rather serious expression on his face. "I had just finished cleaning the shitters at Crumpburger headquarters when your father told me how he had helped you dodge the draft. You know I will never forget what he said to me as I stood in his office with my plunger in one hand and a shitrag in the other. Only the little people go to war, Merv, Crumps never do."

"Trenton, that's something you need to jot in your notepad. And you should take this down as well. Rules are for fukkers with no money, in the US of A, us rich folks can do as we fukkin well please," laughed Crump, and Tribianka clapped and giggled as well. "Mind you, there have been Crumps embroiled in every conflict this nation has fought since the Revolutionary War. You know that it was a Crump who staged the Boston Tea Party by disguising himself as a Native American and tossing all the Britshit tea he could find into Boston Harbor. Of course, a week later, he made a crapload of cash by rebranding it as Crump Tea and selling it to the assmonkeys in the Sons of Liberty at four times the usual price. Some years later, his son paid a bunch of drunken fukkers to dress up as Redcoats and burn down Washington, DC. He then bought up the land at pennies on the dollar and made a killing when the real estate prices rebounded. Then at the Alamo, it was a Crump with a keen eye for making a fast buck who sold the key to the front door of the Mission to General Antonio López de Santa Anna of the Mexican Army, thus ending the 13-day siege. And it was another Crump who started the Spanish-American War of 1898 by supplying the coal that ignited and sank the USS Maine. Though I was told by my father, the dumbass never turned a profit on that fukkin deal."

I listened intently to Crump's history lesson, during which I filled several pages of my notepad with the fascinating details of his family's wartime escapades. However, it quickly became evident to me that in one way or another, throughout the history of the United States, a Crump had tried to profit from each of its wars yet had never taken up arms in its defense.

The American Civil War, in particular, had been exceptionally rewarding for the Crumps. And it would have been more so, Crump sighed, if the dickweasels in the Confederacy had not surrendered after only four short years of fighting. Even though his family had always been bona fide Yankees, this had not stopped them from selling reconditioned Revolutionary War era arms to the South. And while this was undoubtedly a major contributing factor to their defeat, all the same, it made a shitload of cash for one remarkably astute Crump.

During the First World War, Crump grumbled, the fukkers in the US government wanted to intern patriotic German supporting Americans in detention camps, and that included several prominent Crumps. Though they managed to bribe their way to freedom, the unwelcome attention of the Feds in the Crump family businesses meant they regrettably had to sit out this war. Then as luck would have it, a couple of decades later, they got a second chance. With close ties to the German leadership in Berlin, a Crump was able to broker a deal with the Empire of Japan over a Thanksgiving turkey in the year 1941. And I noted, as Crump spluttered and laughed, the dumbshits paid a goddamn million for a worthless aerial photo of some inconsequential fukkin place called Pearl Harbor.

It was Crump's uncle, who, as a golfing partner of Joseph Stalin, made a killing during the Korean War out of buying cheap Russian arms and selling them for top dollar to the Kims. And it was the same uncle a decade or so later that made a deal with the North Vietnamese to construct the Ho Chi Minh trail using POWs instead of paying the locals. Unfortunately for his uncle, it didn't go so well for him during the Cold War, as he was caught selling fake secrets to both Moscow and Washington. Ultimately, he met his end at the hands of a firing squad made up of soldiers from both sides, to the delight of Crump's father, as he was the one to inherit his brother's fortune.

"Trenton, Christopher Columbus may have discovered this fukkin country, but it was us Crumps that made it," proclaimed Crump, as he tweeted his enlightened words to his Crumper followers. "Now, Merv, how are my Space Cowboys coming along?"

"They're doing hunky-dory, Mr. President. In fact, they've just returned from their first mission to construct a Crump-burger in the International Space Station. Naturally, I had them toss out the astronauts' regular food so that they have to eat

Crumpburgers morning, noon, and night. Not that the fukkers can tell what time of day it is during a tour of duty. Anyhow, if they want to eat, then it'll have to be a Crumpburger because there's nothing else but fukkin space up there," chortled the General, while accepting a can of diet coke from Tribianka. "Oh yes, and the automated payment system is working just fine. Every time one of them astronauts makes a purchase, Crumpburger charges their respective government 10 times the price we pay on Earth. That's because of gravity, of course."

The General then paused and explained to me that the United States Space Cowboys, or USSC, was the space service branch of the US Armed Forces. It had been formed by one of Crump's presidential decrees with the mission to boldly go where no fukker has gone before, or so Crump was quoted as saying. Although, in reality, no one had any idea what the fuk the Space Cowboys were supposed to do in space, or anywhere else for that matter. And that included every senior officer in the military and the majority of their subordinates. So, in addition to being the chairman of the Joint Chiefs of Staff, Crump had given the job of chief of space operations to his loyal ex-Vice President of Sanitation, Merv Shizerstrom.

"You know, Merv, I was thinking of sending you up to the International Space Station to ensure their shitters get the full Shizerstrom treatment. The flying fukjob must have been up there for at least 20 years. And I bet in all that time no one has ever bothered to give them a fukkin good cleaning," remarked Crump, who, along with a great many other things, was a well-known germaphobe.

"No need to worry about that, Mr. President. It was the first task my guys undertook after docking with the International Space Station," reassured the General, with a smile. "I personally outfitted every Space Cowboy with a plunger, and they are all equipped with one tank of oxygen and another filled with industrial-strength bleach. Cleaning shitters is an integral part of every Space Cowboy's rigorous training, which, needless to say, is presided over by me. I don't give a shit whether you know how to fly or not, but you've got to be skilled with a plunger, shitrag, and a bottle of bleach to become a Space Cowboy in the US military."

"It sounds like you're doing a fine job, Merv. So what else have you been up to since we last met?" inquired Crump, as he opened another can of diet coke for himself and one for Tribianka.

"Well, these days I spend most of my time at the Pentagon, Mr. President," replied the General, while nodding his head at Crump. "Getting too close to the action plays havoc on my old ticker, and with so many shitters in the building, I'm elbow deep in shit from morning to dusk. Of course, my guys love to blow shit up, so a critical part of my job is to keep the fukkers from blowing the wrong shit up. What I like to do is keep them busy by starting senseless wars with shithole countries that have little to no means of defending themselves. You know that no one gives a crap why we go to war with these fukkin countries, and besides, our own dickfuk people forget we are over there after a couple of news cycles. Out of interest, we're currently staging an offensive against California. It's nothing serious; I just wanted to give those boys in the Navy something to do. So I told them they could take a few potshots at San Francisco, Los Angeles, and their old stomping ground, San Diego."

"Merv, that's fukkin outstanding. The armaments manu-facturers will certainly appreciate your decisive military leadership in boosting their sales, and no doubt that means I'll be getting a larger piece of the action. However, it would be even better if you can get them to bomb the fuk out of the old Governor's Mansion in Sacramento. I want to teach the asswipe that lives there who's numero uno on this crazy fukkin continent," imparted Crump, as he slammed his fist down on the Resolute desk.

"Mr. President, I'll call the Admiral once I get back to the Pentagon. I'm sure he'll be thrilled with the idea and will send a squadron of Hornets up right away," affirmed the General, with a salute. "Trust me; the fukker will never know what has hit him."

"Perfect, Merv," grinned Crump, while tossing his empty can of diet coke onto the floor. "Now, before I take a look at this anti-aircraft gun, there's one more piece of business to discuss. Where are we with Operation Crumpburger?"

"It's progressing better than we planned for, Mr. President," responded the General, who had removed a piece of paper from his jacket pocket. "Crumpburger has now taken over the catering contracts in all branches of the military, and we are currently deploying Crumpburger staff to every US military base on the planet. Within six months, the only food those fukkers will be eating is going to be catered by Crumpburger. The Navy will take a bit longer, but I can assure you that before year's end, every one of their ships will be refitted with a Crumpburger. And, of course, it'll be at the expense of the US taxpayer."

"I never imagined, even in my most sordid dreams that the military would turn out to be such a shitcrazy cash cow. Merv, there's going to be a little something extra in your Christmas bonus this year. Like one of those Hawaiian Islands that keep voting for the fukkin Democrats," beamed Crump, as he rubbed his hands with glee. "So, I think it's about time we headed over to the Rose Garden."

"Daddy, but what about Alaska?" chimed in Tribianka, who was still sitting on Crump's lap with a familiar vacant expression on her face.

"Oh yes, thank you, dear, I forgot about that," admitted Crump, as he retrieved a map of North America from one of the drawers in the Resolute desk and then pointed at the expanse of land labeled, United States. "Merv, I have a problem. We're here, and the big fukker above us is Canada. Then all the way up in the dickfreezing Arctic next to Mother Russia is fukkin Alaska. Fuk knows how it got its statehood, but I guess one of my shitheaded predecessors thought it would be a hoot to have a state that freezes your nuts off year-round. Anyway, Tribianka, who is somewhat of a geography buff, rightfully said to me the other day that it's not really part of the US of A. And so this morning, I made an asskicker of a deal with the Kremlin. They get the land, and in return, Crumpburger won't pay Russia a goddamn dime in taxes for the next 100 years."

"And why is that a problem, Mr. President?" asked the General, who was scrutinizing Crump's map. "You're the President, so you can do as you fukkin well please with this country. If you want to sell a state and the fukkers that live there, then it's entirely up to you. What's more, we've got 48 more of them, so no one will give a fuk about losing a good-for-nothing state like that."

"That's perfectly true, Merv. And if I had sold the fukkers along with the land, then Crumpburger would be paying no taxes to Russia for the next 1,000 years. The problem is that Alaska is a Republican state, and according to my campaign manager, Twatt Jabowsky, I'm going to need their electoral votes if I'm to win a third term in office," explained Crump, while shaking his head. "If only the fukkers had been Democrats, I'd have gladly sold every last one of them. Anyhow, I've already contacted my personal attorney, Shifty Daniels. In his legal opinion, I should annex part of Canada, resettle the fukkers there and call it the State of Alaska. Twatt's onboard with that, and he believes it'll guarantee me three electoral votes in November. I've already got my eye on Vancouver Island, but the assfuk of a Prime Minister up there told me no fukkin way."

"I hear what you're saying, Mr. President. I'll have my guys bomb the fukkers into submission right away," stated the General, as he stood up from the sofa and saluted Crump.

"Merv, that's not going to work. Every year the goddamn Canadians put away a fukload of Crumpburgers. And so I can't risk a protracted conflict that will eat into Crumpburger sales," retorted Crump, who was looking at the map sitting before him. "How about we teach those fukkers a lesson they won't forget in a hurry by launching a tactical nuclear strike on Montreal. Those French-speaking dickrattlers in Quebec have blocked Crumpburger from opening in their province for years, so they deserve to get one of our fukkin nukes right up the ass."

"Nuke them, Daddy, nuke them," giggled Tribianka, as she clapped her hands with joy.

"There you go, Merv. Tribianka likes my idea, so I'll count on you to put Operation Nuke-em into action," confirmed Crump, while glancing at his wristwatch. "Now, I bag the first go of this anti-aircraft gun."

With Crump's military briefing at an end, the four of us marched out of the Oval Office and eagerly made our way to the

Rose Garden. Outside, we were greeted by the sight of newly erected stadium seating that could accommodate 500 paying spectators and a regulation green US Army anti-aircraft gun. Sitting on one of the seats with her feet resting on another and spinning a magnum on one finger was a bored-looking Oleander OnYurway. And grinning like a hyena while placing a shell in the barrel of the anti-aircraft gun was none other than the Crump House press secretary.

"Bich, take your goddamn dickbeaters off that anti-aircraft gun right now," yelled Crump, as he gave her the fukeye. "If you think I'm going to let you take out half of the Crump House with that fukker, then you've got another thing coming."

"Hush ya mouth, Mr. President. I only wanted to make sure it worked," huffed Bich, who then muttered something profane under her breath before taking a seat next to OnYurway.

After the General had given Crump a tour of the anti-aircraft gun and instructed him on how to aim and fire the powerful weapon, Crump looked around the Rose Garden for a target. Seeing a statue of Abraham Lincoln, who he often likened to an oversized fukheaded baboon, he took aim. Then after accepting a pair of earplugs from the General, he fired the gun. Missing his intended target by a mile, Crump shouted, "Fore." And then seconds later, I could see a projectile hit the dome of the Capitol Building.

"Good shot, Daddy," clapped Tribianka, who was standing by Crump's side.

"It's alright, Mr. President. The Senate and Congress are not in session this week," called out Bich, from her front-row seat.

"That's a fukkin pity," sighed Crump, before asking the General to load another shell in the barrel of the anti-aircraft gun. "What I need is a real live target. Bich, where are those undocumented immigrants that were fixing up the East Wing?"

"They've already finished the job and have been deported, Mr. President," replied Bich, who was now standing on her seat to get a better look at the damaged Capitol Building. "I can have OnYurway round up a few of those homeless fukkers if you want, but I daresay it'll take some time."

"Daddy, I've got a better idea," giggled Tribianka, as she whispered something into Crump's ear.

"They'll do," smiled Crump, with a nefarious look in his eyes. "Just tell the useless fukkers they're going on an Easter egg hunt."

About 10 minutes later, Tribianka returned to the Rose Garden, although this time she was accompanied by her two dimwitted brothers. Ronald Crump Jr. was smoking his pipe and wearing a red and black flamenco dress as he walked over to his father. And as usual, Birk was riding his tricycle.

"Hi, Dad, I love a good Easter egg hunt," said Jr., while tapping his pipe and emptying the ashes on Birk's head. "So, where do we start?"

"Go and stand next to the statue of that lameass fukker, Abraham Lincoln. And take your fuknut brother with you," snapped Crump, as he pointed in the direction of his unlucky predecessor located about 200 feet from the anti-aircraft gun.

"I'm going to the Moon," shrieked Birk, while riding his tricycle around the Rose Garden before coming to a halt next to his older brother. Who at that moment was taking a selfie with Abraham Lincoln.

"Stand still, and I'll fukkin send you there," bellowed Crump, while aiming the barrel of the gun at his two sons.

And then, just as Crump was about to fire, Birk pointed at the anti-aircraft gun and screamed, "Space rocket." At which point, he started peddling his tricycle as fast as he could, and his flamenco dress-wearing brother, who was eager to be the first to find an Easter egg, chased after him.

Annoyed that his target had moved, Crump fired the gun anyway. And although the shell missed Birk and Jr., it blew the statue of Abraham Lincoln to smithereens before leaving the grounds of the Crump House and hitting the Washington Monument. Needless to say, with an almighty big bang.

As we watched in awe as the 555-foot marble obelisk toppled to the ground, Crump turned to the General and told him that he'd had all the fun he could take that day. And with that, the chairman of the Joint Chiefs of Staff picked up the toolbox containing his trusty plunger and a bottle of industrial-strength bleach. Then after a brief salute, he quick marched his way back to the Crump House and dutifully stepped into the first shitter he came across.

6

CRUMP on Religion

"I've never had any time for religion. Only fukwits believe in shit like that!"

— Ronald S. Crump, President of the United States

* * *

"Ah, Trenton, you're here at last. What was the name of that dickwad who created the world in seven days?" asked Crump, who was sitting at the Resolute desk with a can of diet coke in one hand and a cell phone in the other.

"I think you must be referring to God," I replied, upon entering the Oval Office and taking a seat next to Crump.

"That's the fukker," nodded Crump, while tweeting something to his followers that I assumed must have been more of his insightful words of wisdom. "It's been on the tip of my fukkin tongue all morning, but for the life of me, I just couldn't remember his goddamn name. Trenton, except for Tribianka's wedding, I've never set foot in a church, and I never will. You know why? Because God was a dumbass Democrat, that's why.

That shitbagger claimed he made the world in seven days for everyone, but if the fukker had been a Republican, he would have kept all the assholes out."

During our lunch, which as usual entailed eating several Crumpburgers and as much diet coke as I could drink, Crump spoke at length about the stupidity of religion and how he was thinking of banning it. As I wrote his enlightened words in my notepad, he turned on the television so that we could listen to the SHITE buddies' shitwag before our first meeting of the day. To Crump's delight and obvious amusement, Prick Enderbee was ranting about the destruction of the Washington Monument. Although, interestingly, he made no mention of the historic structure being hit by a shell from an anti-aircraft gun fired from the grounds of the Crump House. Instead, the irate SHITE buddie claimed the monument's collapse was entirely due to the fact it had been erected by a Democrat. And this, he insisted, was another reason why anyone thinking of voting for Smilin' Mo Fudrucker over Crump had to be a no-good shitbrained loser.

"Slap ya pappy, Mr. President," called out Bich Landers, as she confidently strode into the Oval Office with Oleander OnYurway by her side. "The General sure did a fine job with the Crump House shitters. They're so goddamn clean I'm afraid to use them for anything aside from snackin' on redneck caviar and my afternoon nap. That's why I spent the mornin' diggin' a hole in the Rose Garden with my legs crossed. Now OnYurway and I can do our business the way Granny always does back in Arkansas."

"Bich, you know that I only keep you around to make me money and to ensure I get re-elected for a third term. If you want to spend your time digging fukkin holes, then I'll have OnYurway kick your worthless ass all the way back to the fukhole you came from," snapped Crump, while throwing a Crumpburger at Bich. "Now, there's money to be made by building a new Washington Monument, so I've decided to award myself the contract. I'll also be renaming it the Crump Monument because George Washington was just a dickswinging fukhead. And this time, I want it to look like one of those pyramids the pharaohs built, but it's got to be at least double the size of the biggest fukker they completed. It's a pity you had those undocumented immigrants deported. Oh well, there's plenty more cheap labor where they came from, so round up as many of them as you and OnYurway can get your hands on and have the asswipes start immediately. You can put the fukkers on the same contract as the last lot so that they won't cost me a penny. And you can tell those lazy assclowns in the Secret Service they're going to supervise the construction, just like the overseers did back in Ancient Egypt."

"Sure will do, Mr. President," saluted Bich, with a broad grin. "Although I can probably have the fukkers who rebuilt the East Wing start tomorrow. That's because every undocumented immigrant deported by ICE always manages to sneak back into the country within a matter of days. One of ya predecessors built a fukass wall across the southern border to stop 'em. But all that did was make it more difficult for Americans to flee to Mexico. That one-term cockbite was a real dumbfuk; he didn't realize most undocumented immigrants fly here like almost everyone else. Anyhows, these days, ICE electronically tags all deportees to make it easier for them to catch the fukkers when they return. They're probably all sittin' in some fukhouse detention center as we speak, so all it will take is a phone call from me to have 'em delivered to the Crump House sometime during the night."

"Then make it so, Bich," nodded Crump, while handing his press secretary a can of diet coke. For no other reason than she was back in his good fukkers book once again. "So, what do you have for me today?"

"Well, Mr. President, the fukkers in the fake press have been assbadgerin' me all mornin' about the Washington Monument. They're not buyin' our story that an earthquake caused it to topple over yesterday afternoon. I've arranged a press briefin' with the Crump House press corps at 3.30 to shitwag with the fukkers, and it would be best if ya made an appearance as well. Ya can even talk about ya pyramid because that's sure to distract the fukkin jackasses," stated Bich, as she opened her Crump House press diary. "And the only other thing ya need to concern ya'self with today is a campaign meetin' with Twatt Jabowsky in 30 minutes."

"Right, I'll give those fukkers in the fake press what for. But for the next half hour, the four of us are going to play a game of Twister," declared Crump, who was signaling to Bich to set up the game. "And OnYurway, lose the magnums this time because I don't want you shooting up the Oval Office and hitting Trenton and me."

Around forty-five minutes later, our second game of Twister was interrupted by a solitary yet rather loud thud originating from the other side of the Oval Office door. As Crump declared himself the winner, even though he had been the first to fall, I stood up and walked to the other end of the office, then opened the door to investigate. What I saw was a visibly inebriated Twatt Jabowsky flailing around on his back with a jug of Kentucky moonshine in his hand and official-looking papers strewn all over the floor.

"Fuk! Who slammed that goddamn door in my face," complained Twatt, as he rubbed his head. I then helped the burly man reeking of moonshine and cheap cigars to his feet before retrieving the papers he had been carrying. Then seeing Crump, who was now seated at the Resolute desk with his arms folded, give his campaign manager the fukeye, I guided the drunkard to the sofa where he took a hefty swig from his jug. "Ah, that's better. There's nothing like a good belt of Kentucky moonshine to calm your nerves and straighten your head."

"So, Twatt, what do you want with me? You goddamn incompetent pisshead. Time is money, and I'm a busy man, so this better be good," thundered Crump, who was motioning to OnYurway to return the Twister mat and spinner to its box. And then all of us except Crump joined the Crump campaign manager on the sofa.

"You know after all the rigmarole with that fukkin door, I plumb forgot, but let me check my notes and get back to you, Mr. President," shrugged Twatt, as he gulped down more of the moonshine while running his eyes over the papers I had just handed him. "Anyone want to join me?"

"Granny always says ya'd have to be dumber than a turkey to turn down an offer of a jug of hooch," exclaimed Bich, who grabbed hold of the jug before any of us could stop her. Then, after making eye contact with Crump, OnYurway pointed one of her magnums at the Crump House press secretary. Whereby, I took the opportunity to return the dangerously heady beverage to Twatt Jabowsky.

"Ah, I remember now. I've got it all written down here," chuckled Twatt, while waving his papers in the air. "Mr. President, you need to start your training regimen for the SPATs so that you're ready to take on Smilin' Mo Fudrucker. As you know, half the fukkers in the country are going to be following them. And, naturally, they'll expect the next President of the US of A to be the victor, as you were before the last two elections."

As I was the only one in the room who was not privy to what Crump's campaign manager was referring to, Twatt spent the next few minutes explaining everything a presidential intern needed to know about the SPATs. Previously, debates had been the norm before every presidential election since the first debate between Senator John F. Kennedy and Vice President Tricky Dicky Nixon. These came to an unexpected and rather abrupt end after the 45th president made a complete fukwit of himself and went asscrazy on-air during the 2020 election year. Then after taking a series of cognitive assessments that determined he not only had an IQ of 72 but was also barking mad, the debates were abandoned in favor of a series of tests to reflect the qualities the American public expected in a US president.

The Standardized Presidential Aptitude Tests, or SPATs as they had become known, were developed to determine the best presidential candidate using three carefully chosen criteria. First, came the intelligence round, which entailed a 60-minute quiz of 8th-grade trivia questions because that was deemed the level of learning a president would need. Then the second round concerned a candidate's strength, and this required the two of them to arm-wrestle, with the winner being the one who won two contests out of three. Finally, the last round was all about agility and speed, which consisted of 13 games of snap in honor of the original English colonies.

"Twatt, you should know by now that Smilin' Mo Fudrucker could never beat me," bragged Crump, as he crushed an empty can of diet coke in his hands in a vain attempt to demonstrate his superior strength.

"Of course, Mr. President. But all the same, I'd be happier if you spent some time with OnYurway to work on your arm wrestling technique and practice your snap game with Trib-ianka. And for the quiz, I've already instructed Skeeter to get his hands on a copy of the questions, just like last time. So you've got nothing to worry about there. I'll have my top people work on the answers, and then we'll feed them to you using a concealed earpiece during the first round of the SPATs," winked Twatt, while lighting a cigar.

"What about that sanctimonious walking dickstick, Mylo Peckerhead?" demanded Crump, who was pointing his finger at Twatt Jabowsky. "That fukker has to go up against LSD, and for what it's worth, I've got zero confidence in the inept asshead."

"Luckily for us, Mr. President, the vice presidential SPATs don't have an intelligence round, as brains are not a require-ment for that fukkin job. If they did, then we'd certainly be fukked because the Vice President is a real dickwit," answered Twatt, as he finished off the last of his moonshine. "I can have him practice his snap game, but when it comes to arm wrestling, I think LSD is going to do a real fukjob on him. Our best bet is if I have Skeeter hire someone to break her goddamn wrestling arm."

"Good idea, Twatt," nodded Crump, who was watching his intoxicated campaign manager shake the jug he was still holding. "So, do you have anything else for me, or are you just going to sit there all afternoon and wazz into your fukkin jug?"

"Now you mention it, Mr. President, I could do with a quick wazz, and it appears my jug is empty. A jug of moonshine doesn't seem to last as long as it used to. Oh well, I always keep a spare one in my office over in the East Wing, so I'll call it a day," yawned Twatt, while getting to his feet. And then, for the second time that afternoon, he stumbled headlong into the Oval Office door.

After I had given Twatt Jabowsky a helping hand to get him to his feet once again and led him into the corridor, I pointed in the direction of his office before the confused sothead tottered away. Then after killing the next half hour drinking more diet coke and watching SHITE news, the four of us made our way to the Fukkers Briefing Room to meet with the Crump House press corps.

"Y'all fukkers, Bich is in the house, so shut ya goddamn yappin'," yelled Bich, to quieten the rowdy members of the press corps sitting before her. Then, after giving us all a truly awful rendition of Crump is Simply the Best, she spit the shit for a few minutes before opening the briefing to questions.

"Rumors are circulating that claim the Washington Monument was hit by an anti-aircraft shell fired from the grounds of the Crump House yesterday afternoon," shouted out Stoner McCall from SBC, who had recently been allowed back into the press corps after his much-publicized suspension. "But the Crump House press release asserts the monument collapsed due to a magnitude 12 earthquake. However, according to the US Geological Survey, the nearest earthquake occurred over 2,000 miles away, and the highest magnitude ever recorded for an earthquake was 9.5. And that mothafukker took place in Chile over half a century ago. So what do you have to say about that, Bich?"

"First of all, fuk you, Stoner," screamed Bich, and then with her thumb in the air, she turned to give Crump a grin. "What do those fukheads at the US Geological Survey know anyway?

They're just a bunch of lefty Democrat votin' dickslappers. If ya want the real facts and not the fake ones, then ya need to watch SHITE news."

At that point in the briefing, Vaj Ingersol of the SHITE buddies chimed in and spoke at length about the pile of rubble that had been the Washington Monument. She claimed SHITE news had exclusive access to an eyewitness, who, at the time of the catastrophe, happened to be innocently shooting his licensed firearm into the air as he walked through the grounds of the National Mall. While she could not name him for fear of retribution by the left-wing deep state, he had told her that just as sure as Jesus was a blonde-haired white guy with blues eyes, the ground had shuddered under his feet only seconds before the marble obelisk tumbled to the ground. Then, she added, if it had been built by a Republican administration, the fukkin thing would still be standing.

As the Fukkers Briefing Room erupted into a whole load of jeering and scrunched paper throwing, OnYurway took it upon herself to fire her magnums into the air. While this succeeded in subduing almost everyone in the room, Jem Tossa entered into a heated exchange with Vaj Ingersol by calling her a bullshitting twatlipped cumbubble. Thankfully, though, this brief war of words ended somewhat abruptly, with Crump's senior counselor pistol-whipping the NBS reporter before dragging him kicking and screaming from the room.

Now that a semblance of order had been temporarily regained, Stoner McCall courageously got to his feet and waved one of his hands in the air. Then after he made eye contact with the Crump House press secretary again, he apprehensively asked her another contentious question, "So what's that big fukker of an anti-aircraft gun doing in the Rose Garden?"

"Stoner, I'm glad ya asked me that question because the way thin's are lookin', most of ya fukkers in the fake press are likely gonna get a closer look at it sooner or later. Though, for now, it's on a national security need-to-know basis. And shitshovelers like you lot, don't fukkin need to know," scoffed Bich, while pulling out her Arkansas toothpick and pointing it at the mistrustful members of the press corps. "Now, the President would like to announce a new initiative that is not only goin' to create jobs for a bunch of idle dicksneezes, but it will also become a shinin' beacon of light in this country of whinin' shitbags."

Following a few moments of applause from Bich, OnYurway, and Vaj Ingersol, Crump stood up and walked to the podium. Immediately, he launched into an expletive-laden tirade regarding the fake press and how he would like to round up every lying reporter in the country and let OnYurway and her magnums loose on them. Needless to say, his vitriolic comments did not include SHITE news and the honest Republican supporting men and women who worked there.

Then after listening to Crump rant on for a good 10 minutes about undocumented immigrants, the Posse, and his new pet hate, the fukkin Canadians, I made a sign resembling a triangle with my fingers to remind him that he was there to talk about his pyramid. So with a nod and a wink, Crump announced his grand plan to construct a new monument where the old one previously stood. Although this time, it was not going to be named after a no-good toothless dumbass. Instead, it was to honor the greatest president the country has ever elected. And that, of course, was Ronald S. Crump.

Once Crump had finished speaking, Mallory Hightower of CPR cried out, "Mr. President, would it not be construed by

95

the American public as rather vain, even for you, to rename the Washington Monument, the Crump Monument?"

"Listen, Mallory, the fukkers out there need to move with the times. I'm the boss in this fukkin town, and that means we're going to have an asskicker of a pyramid erected in the middle of the National Mall with my name on it," responded Crump, while giving me a thumbs up. "And this mothafukker isn't going to take 20 years to construct, unlike the ones built in Egypt. It's going to be finished by my next inauguration day. Although you don't need to bother yourself with that because by the look of you, you'll probably be six feet under by then. Now, do you shitwaggers have any other questions before I clock off for the day?"

"Yes, Mr. President, I have a question," hollered Raz Alvarez of DNN, who was sitting at the back of the room in the misbehaving fukkers section. "This morning in Rome, the Pope made an off-the-cuff remark to a group of reporters. He said that there's more chance of Team USA winning the World Cup than Crump stepping foot in a church. What I would like to know, is do you have any comment for your evangelical base?"

"Raz, and all you other assmonkeys sitting here, I can guarantee there's no fukker living in this country that's more religious than Crump," thundered Crump, as he slammed his fists down on the podium. "That's why Jesus voted for me in the last two elections, and I have it on good authority he will do so again. His Dad may have been a lameass slacker by taking seven days to create the world when I could have easily done it in five. But everyone knows if he was still around, then he'd also vote for Crump because it says so in that goddamn book the evangelicals are always touting."

"Crump, it's called the Bible," yelled Loudmouth Lonnie

Laverty from SBC, who, just like Raz Alvarez, was seated in the misbehaving fukkers section due to his previous altercation with Bich Landers. "So, if you're so religious, what denomination are you? And when was the last time you attended a church service?"

Unfortunately for the outspoken SBC reporter, he had not learned his lesson that bitchassin in a Crump House press briefing was never a wise thing to do. So, in no more than a blink of an eye, holding her Arkansas toothpick in one hand, Bich jumped to her feet and ran to confront Crump's antagonizer. Then as Loudmouth Lonnie Laverty and the Crump House press secretary hotfooted their way around the room, OnYurway fired her magnums into the air.

As outright pandemonium took hold in the Fukkers Briefing Room, the only thing for Crump and me to do was to make a hasty retreat. After grabbing hold of Crump's arm, I led him to the door posthaste. And then we made our escape with a heavily armed detachment of Secret Service agents protecting our rear. Once the two of us had entered the safety of the Oval Office, we collapsed onto the sofa. Then laughing, Crump opened a can of diet coke for himself and offered a second can to me before announcing, not surprisingly, that we should call it a day.

I did not see Crump again until lunchtime the following day when I walked into the Oval Office to witness him throwing Crumpburgers at the television and raving about the fukkers in the fake press. What had irked him, I was soon to find out, was that a distraught Mylo Peckerhead had called him earlier to say he should turn on his television right away. Then after his Vice President told him to take a look at what the devil-worshipping Satanists at SBC were saying about him that day, the incensed Crump had gone and blown his proverbial gasket.

"Trenton, listen to the shit these assbenders on SBC have been spouting all morning," bellowed Crump, as I listened to Loudmouth Lonnie Laverty interview a group of Crump-supporting evangelicals wearing ASS caps. "The fukkers are claiming that since I took over the presidency, no one has seen me attend any fukkin church or goddamn religious event. And not only that, they're saying there is no evidence I currently belong to any kissass religious denomination or ever have."

"Um, but isn't that all true?" I asked, as I helped myself to a Crumpburger.

"Of course, it's true. The point is we don't want the ignorant fukkers out there believing that it's true, especially not the fukkin evangelicals," explained Crump, who was opening a can of diet coke as I ate my Crumpburger. "As you know, Trenton, I rely upon a voter base of uniformed shitheaded religious morons who think I believe in all that bullcrap. You know me, I'll tell the fukkers whatever they want to hear as long as they vote Crump and keep eating Crumpburgers. Telling the nagasses the truth, that Ronald S. Crump believes religion is for asscrazy dicksticks, is not only bad for business, but it's the last thing we need in the run-up to an election."

While I took a bite out of my second Crumpburger, Crump became even more enraged as he channel hopped from SBC to CPR, then to NBS, and finally DNN. Seeing that every fake news channel was talking about Crump and questioning his devotion to any kind of religion, I took it upon myself to retrieve the remote control from his outstretched hand. Then within seconds of me switching the channel to the trusted folks at SHITE news, Crump calmed down to the point where we could make a plan.

Knowing his pretense to be religious meant money for Crumpburger and votes for Crump, we agreed that an emergency campaign meeting should be convened that very afternoon. As I called Bich Landers to round up Oleander OnYurway and Twatt Jabowsky, Crump picked up the phone and spoke to his most senior advisor. Within the hour, we heard two knocks on the Oval Office door. And then Tribianka walked in, followed by Bich, OnYurway, and a jittery-looking Waywerd Pushover.

"Where's Twatt?" barked Crump, as he peered at the four new arrivals standing before him.

"The fukker was layin' out last night again. So we won't see him for a day or two," answered Bich, who was referring to the fact that Twatt Jabowsky had spent the evening and early morning hours partying with a jug of Kentucky moonshine and was now in his bed sleeping it off.

"Typical, the useless scrotelicking sot is never around when I need him," fumed Crump, while giving his son-in-law the fukeye. "And what are you doing here, Waywerd? If you've come to assbadger me again, then you can turn around and go back to whatever fukkin place you've been hiding."

"Hi, Dad," waved Waywerd, with a forced grin. "I heard about your little problem, and as the Crump House chief of staff, I'm here to offer you my extensive expertise in matters such as these."

"It's, Mr. President, to you, and what the fuk does an asskissing dickweasel like you know about religion?" hissed Crump, as he gestured to Tribianka to come and sit on his lap. "Trenton, this is the fukker who was an hour late to his own fukkin wedding. And why? Because he couldn't find the humungous fukbanger of a cathedral that I rented only two blocks from his goddamn apartment."

"But, Dad, at college, I was the President of the Harvard

chapter of Hare Krishna. So unless Trenton was an ardent churchgoer back in England, then that makes me the most religious person in the room," professed Waywerd, who was being uncharacteristically assertive as he spoke to Crump.

"Hare fukkin Krishna! Waywerd, are you giving me the fukaround? If it was left to you, then Asyphilis, Tribianka, and I would have to attend a fukkin church service every week. And we would even have to sing those goddamn religious hymns," raged Crump, while picking up a Crumpburger and throwing it at his trembling son-in-law. "Trenton, do you have much experience with religion in England?"

"Not really. Like myself, the majority of the English are not very religious, to say the least," I replied, with a shrug of the shoulders. "We do have the Church of England, but they only stay in business by offering a one-hour service with bread and wine right before the pubs open."

"Granny is religious," chimed in Bich, to Crump's displeasure. "She likes most religions, but for some reason that none of us in the family can fathom, they don't all like her. A few years back, she invited a bunch of Jewish and Muslim families to a good ol' Arkansas hog roast, and ya know what, that was the last she ever saw of 'em. It was the same when a family of Hindus bought a farm on the other side of the creek. Granny greeted 'em with a crock of her famous cow brain stew, and they upped and left without as much as a howdy-do and thank you. The one she doesn't get alon' with is run by those uptight evangelicals as they always get in a tizzy when ya talk to 'em about abortions. You know, Granny says that if a gal can't have an abortion every now and again, then how's she ever going to take a vacation from spittin' out young'uns. I can tell ya, she's tried out more religions than I've had possum fritters.

Although nowadays she's settled on Buddhism because like Granny, them fukkers just don't give a shit."

Once Bich saw that Crump was giving her the fukeye, she wisely shut up and sat down on the sofa, and so did the rest of us. Meanwhile, Tribianka was still seated on Crump's lap and was clapping as she listened to the SHITE buddies' shitwag about a wholly fictitious story regarding a religiously devout Crump. Then all of a sudden, Crump launched into one of his profanity-strewn rants about religion before telling us there were far too many isms in this goddamn country he ruled. It was at that moment I came up with an idea to solidify the religious vote behind Crump while ensuring he would never have to become a real church-going evangelical.

"In England, 500 years ago, Henry VIII had a problem with religion," I disclosed, with a can of diet coke in my hand. "He had a falling out with the Pope because he wanted to have a new wife every other year while the Catholic Church insisted he had to stick with the first one. So being that he was the king, and he could do as he bloody well pleased, Henry nationalized the churches and pocketed all their money. Then he made himself the head of his own Church and got himself a new wife every time he chopped the head off the old one. So, what I'm thinking is why don't you do the same and make a decree declaring Crumpism the national religion of the United States."

"Trenton, I like it, I like it a lot," beamed Crump, just as Tribianka gave a gleeful squeal. "I can take over every church, temple, mosque, and whatever else these religious nutjobs call their places of worship and convert them into Crumpburgers. If the fukkers want to pray, then they can buy a Crumpburger while they're going about it. And if they want one of those fukkin confessions, then I'll charge them extra."

"But, Dad, what about the Hare Krishnas?" blurted Waywerd, who had his hand held high in the air. "I can tell you that the International Society of Krishna Consciousness is not going to like this one little bit. And as their sole representative in the Crump House, I must formally object."

"Who gives a shit what you and the Hare Krishnas like or don't like," retorted Crump, just as OnYurway pulled out one of her magnums and pointed it at Waywerd Pushover's shaking head. "I'll have Mylo Peckerhead deal with his fellow evangelicals by offering them a free Crumpburger to convert. And if any other religious fukker has a problem with Crumpism, then I can always have them deported. Naturally, I'll be the head of our nation's new national religion, but I don't want to have to lift a finger to run it, so I'll need some fukker to do all the work."

"How about you name someone to be Archbishop?" I suggested, while nodding my head. "That's how it works in the Church of England. The Queen is the head of the whole caboodle, and she has some costumed halfwit run it for her."

"Well, I've got plenty of worthless fukkers working for me to choose from," pondered Crump, who was helping himself to another can of diet coke.

"What about that old dickswinger, Dwight Jacoff?" proposed Bich, while cleaning her fingernails with her trusty Arkansas toothpick. "He's always hangin' around the Crump House pissassin' it up with Twatt Jabowsky."

"Archbishop Dwight Jacoff it is then. Bich, you tell that shittosser, I want to see him in the Oval Office without delay," affirmed Crump, as he gave a rather loud and lengthy yawn before smiling and pointing his finger at me. "Trenton, that'll stick it to those fukkers who said I'm not religious."

7

CRUMP on Education

"I never had the need for a goddamn education. I was born knowing everything!"
— Ronald S. Crump, President of the United States

* * *

"They shat their pants, Mr. President. Just like ya said they would," announced Bich Landers, as she charged into the Oval Office with Oleander OnYurway in tow.

While I polished off my second Crumpburger and drank my fill of diet coke, the breathless Crump House press secretary blurted something unintelligible about the fukkin Canadians. Then waving a printout of a top-secret communication from the chairman of the Joint Chiefs of Staff, she helped herself to my can of diet coke before disclosing what had gone down.

To Crump's quite obvious delight, Operation Nuke-em had been a complete and overwhelming success. In fact, the Canadian Government had caved in and agreed to Crump's demands without the US military having to launch a single nuclear warhead. According to the General, the mere mention of a tactical nuclear strike on Montreal had brought the fukkers in the North to their knees. At which point, Crump interrupted his press secretary to explain to me that this successful I win-you lose negotiation tactic was a major contributing factor to his success.

As I jotted this down in my notepad, in the section I had named, The Art of Doing Business the Crump Way, Bich continued with her impromptu briefing. Now that Vancouver Island had been annexed to the US of A and renamed Alaska, the General had instructed the US Army to clear out every Canadian squatter. This left the Crump House with only one thing to do before handing the former State of Alaska over to the Russians. And that was to shitwag some kind of asscrazy justification to forcibly remove its residents and resettle the fukkers on Vancouver Island.

"Trenton, that's international diplomacy, Crump style," laughed Crump, who was helping himself to another can of diet coke. "And Bich, you can tell all those fukkers in Alaska we're relocating them further south because of global warming. It'll make the goddamn doomsayers think I actually believe in all that bullcrap and should stop the shitbrained scientists from assbadgering me for a while. Oh yes, and if you get the fukaround from that jagoff governor of theirs, then tell her that we've discovered gold on Vancouver Island, so she'll need to bring her fukkin prospecting pan and shovel."

Since the emergency campaign meeting which had taken place in the Oval Office the previous week, Crump had already issued his first religious decree while on-air with the SHITE buddies. After telling them the country was to have a national religion called Crumpism, he was summarily applauded by Vaj

Ingersol, Dicker Polson, and Ranting Prick Enderbee. Then, not unexpectedly, following his announcement that he would head the new religion himself, Crump received a rapturous standing ovation from the three asslicking hosts.

Two days after Crump's appearance on the SHITE buddies, Dwight Jacoff had been ordained as Crumpism's first arch-bishop. But not before Ronald Crump Jr. had designed and tailored the archbishop's requisite silly costume decked out with a Crumpburger logo on the front and back. The ceremony took place in the Oval Office and was a typical Crump House affair that was officiated by Crump, while Tribianka, Bich, and I looked on as OnYurway pointed both her magnums at Dwight Jacoff's perspiring head.

It was a part-time pro bono job for the downtrodden Jacoff as Crump was unwilling to pay him so much as a shitgreased penny. Well, not for dressing up like a goddamn dickmeister and mumbling a bunch of assbrained words that only a pis-sant fukwizard could possibly comprehend. Besides, he was already employed as Crumpburger's Vice President of Quality, a position he had held for over 20 years. And in this job, he had the thankless responsibility of ensuring each Crumpburger contained the cheapest beef money could buy and, needless to say, a whole load of BSE.

Meanwhile, as Crump reviewed the proposals for his pyramid, thousands of undocumented immigrants were flown in from detention centers around the country. They were now camped in the grounds of the National Mall, and their days were spent removing the rubble from the site of the old Washington Monument. It was indisputably a sight to behold as the lucky fukkers worked around the clock in 12-hour shifts, seven days a week, with one afternoon off once a month. With

Crumpburger providing the catering and the 100,000 volt shock-stick wielding Secret Service agents overseeing the project, all that was required now was for Crump to select the design he liked the most.

"Bich, I've got three kickass pyramid proposals for the Crump Monument sitting on the Resolute Desk. Trenton and I have already chosen the best. If you can tell us which one it is, then I won't shitcan you just yet," taunted Crump, while giving me a wink.

"Well, I'm sure Granny would go for the biggest fukker, so that's the one I'd pick," grinned Bich, as she inspected each of the designs and pointed to the one that looked like a Mayan temple.

"It looks like you'll be the Crump House press secretary for another week after all," chuckled Crump, who, as the winner of our bet, had his hand outstretched for the dollar I owed him.

The chosen design was indeed the largest of the three. And it would accommodate not only a 3,000 seat Crumpburger but also the aptly named Church of Crump, which is where Archbishop Dwight Jacoff would reside. As the seat of Crumpism and the largest Crumpburger in the world, the Crump Monument would feature red Crumpburger neon signs on each of the pyramid's four sides. Then if that wasn't enough to beguile the residents of Washington, DC and its visitors, the apex of the pyramid was to be topped off with a 24 Karat gold statue of Crump.

On top of his day job, Archbishop Dwight Jacoff was tasked with the dissolution of every religious place of worship in the 49 states and their conversion to Crumpburgers. The managers of these new establishments would also double as ministers of the Church of Crump, who, naturally, would have to pledge their devotion to Crump. Not only would this mean higher Crumpburger sales, but Crump would also be able to charge a fee for religious dispensations for things like adultery and downloading porn. And to Crump's exultation, as a bona fide religious organization, this business venture, including every new Crumpburger, would be entirely exempt from all forms of taxation.

"Mr. President, the fukkers in the fake press claim ya impingin' on every American's right to freedom of religion as guaranteed by the fukkin First Amendment," stated Bich, who was reading from the notes in her Crump House dairy. "And the goddamn Vatican has requested you declare Catholicism this country's official religion. In return, they say the Pope will make you a livin' saint."

"Interesting idea, but as the head of Crumpism, I can make myself a saint any time I fukkin well want. Isn't that right, Trenton?" retorted Crump, as I nodded my head in agreement. "And I don't give a flying assfuk what those fukkers in the fake press say as I decide what goes down in this shitass country, not a document written over 200 years ago by a fraternity of cockass fukwits. Now, I understand Tribianka is waiting for Trenton and me in the Beast because I'm supposed to visit some shithole of a public school this afternoon."

"That's right, Mr. President. Ya gonna be handin' out Little Fukker meals and givin' a motivational speech to the fukkin young'uns at Benedict Arnold Elementary School," acknowledged Bich, with a grin. "OnYurway and I will be accompanyin' ya along with a photographer and camera team to record the event. Smilin' Mo Fudrucker and LSD are always talkin' about the merits of education on the campaign trail. So the goal of this school visit is to make it look like ya really do give a shit about education."

Fifteen minutes later, the presidential motorcade pulled out of the Crump House with Crump, Tribianka, and I sitting in the Beast drinking diet coke and watching SHITE news. Thankfully, the fake press had not been invited as Crump didn't want to answer any of their dumbfuk questions that day. And this meant we were traveling in an unusually small motorcade consisting of a dozen cars, two buses holding around 100 heavily armed Secret Service agents, and six Bradley Fighting vehicles. As a matter of course, SWAT teams were positioned along our route, and snipers had their gun sights trained on the school. Just in case any of the 5 to 12-year-olds got out of hand.

"Daddy, I've never been to a public school before," remarked Tribianka, who was sitting on Crump's lap. "Are they anything like finishing schools?"

"No, only fukkin losers attend public schools. They'd be better off calling them shithole schools as we're probably going to need tetanus shots after visiting this one," complained Crump, while shaking his head. "The Republican Party believes the American dream is to pay for your own goddamn education, but for some reason, the dumbass electorate disagrees. Not that Republicans give a shit what voters want, which is why they always vote to cut the education budget every year."

It was around 2.30 when the presidential motorcade entered Benedict Arnold Elementary, located in a somewhat run-down suburb of Washington, DC. Without delay, the Secret Service and every one of the Bradley Fighting Vehicles took up defensive positions throughout the school. Then once the Secret Service was happy that the school was secure, Crump, Tribianka, and I exited the Beast under the watchful eye of Oleander OnYurway and her fully loaded magnums.

While I remained close to the Beast, Crump and Tribianka were greeted by a welcoming committee comprised of Principal Homer Boggs, who thankfully was an ardent Crumper, and several members of the school faculty. Choosing to live dangerously, for once, Crump shook Principal Boggs's hand, but not before pulling on a pair of surgical gloves, and Tribianka did the same. With the initial formalities at an end, we made our way inside and then entered the school gym where Bich Landers and the Crump House press team were waiting to film Crump in all his majestic glory.

Two years ago, Crump had issued a decree that every public school in the land must open a Crumpburger. So I was not surprised in the least to see a mountain of Little Fukker meals sitting on the stage. As Bich yelled, "Action!" the camera started rolling, then Crump and his most senior advisor got down to business. With 1,000 hungry children, who had not been fed since breakfast, lined up in the hallways, Secret Service agents sprayed them with disinfectant before they were allowed to enter the gym. Then as quickly as they could, Crump and Tribianka handed each of the starving kids their long-overdue lunch before OnYurway shooed them to an empty table.

"Whoa! I was sweatin' like a two-bit hooker in church, Mr. President. Though I reckon it went as well as can be expected," exclaimed Bich, who had climbed onto the stage just as Crump and Tribianka dished out the last of the Little Fukkers. "They sure are an ugly bunch of critters, but the voters love this sort of shit, so I'll have SHITE news run the video every day from now till the election. All that's left for ya to do is give your goddamn speech and answer some fukkin questions. And before we leave, I'll have the photographer take a few shots of ya with some of the young'uns."

"Bich, just make sure none of them are fatties. You know that I hate having my photo taken with fat fukkers because they always make me look fatter than I really am," grumbled Crump, while disposing of his surgical gloves before spraying alcohol on his hands and face. "Trenton, you should take note of that by jotting this down. Never have a photo taken with a lardass. Period!"

"There's no need for ya to worry, Mr. President. Bich's got everythin' under control. And I've personally picked out the best lookin' shitlin's I could find to make ya look good," reassured Bich, as she gave Crump a grin and a double thumbs-up. "Diversity is what the voters want to see, and so I've chosen a girl, two boys, and a fukkin transgender Asian kid. And to score some more points with the goddamn liberal undecideds, OnYurway will stick the fukker in a wheelchair. The others include a black kid, although I had to blacken her face for the camera, a sombrero-wearin' Mexican, and I'm dressin' another to look like a fukkin Native American. My brother Cooter supplied the eagle feather and buckskin for his outfit, and Jr. even loaned us one of his pipes. So if ya ask me, that one sure is gonna look like the real dickswingin' McCoy."

Once the students at Benedict Arnold Elementary had finished their lunch of Little Fukkers and were seen playing with the cheapshit toys that came with every meal, Crump stood up to begin his speech. He started by shitwagging a few lines of heartfelt bullcrap about how the health and wellbeing of every fukkin poor kid in the nation had always been of the utmost importance to him. He then bragged that this was the impetus for the Crump administration to close the godawful cockroach-infested public school cafeterias and replace them with Crumpburgers. At which point, Crump congratulated himself on coming up with the idea of a nutritional kids meal before urging his captive audience to eat Little Fukkers at least three times a day.

He rounded his speech off with a Crump interpretation of the tale of the three little pigs. In Crump's version of the fabled story, the first two pigs were just nickel-and-dime assheaded fukkers that could only afford to buy shithouses made of straw and wood. The third pig, on the other hand, was an exceptionally clever billionaire who lived in a palace built of 24 karat gold bricks, and his name happened to be Crump. Both the straw and wooden houses were burnt down by a fire-breathing dragon called LSD, and then their occupants were eaten by a big bad wolf named Fudrucker. This left only Crump, the filthy rich pig, who, because he had piles of cash, was able to live happily ever after in his palace made of fireproof gold bricks. The moral of this story, Crump claimed, was that money means everything, and no one gives a shit about losers that don't have a fukkin dime to their name.

"That speech sure did inspire the hell out of me, Mr. President. Kids, let's have an asscrackin' round of applause for the leader of the free world, Ronald S. Crump," yelled Bich, who had climbed back onto the stage and was standing beside Crump. "Now, before we depart for the Crump House, the President will be happy to answer a few questions."

"When I'm all grown up, I want to be just like you, Mr. President. So what advice would you give me if I was to stand for the highest office in the land?" asked a chubby nine-year-old kid sitting closest to Crump.

"Fuk me, are you trying to jerk me off or something?" replied Crump, as he turned to me and rolled his eyes before silently mouthing the words, fat fukker. "Listen to me, jelly belly, you'll

111

never amount to anything because you're fat, undoubtedly dumb, and you have to be shitfukking poor to be attending this school. All that you can hope for is a job at Crumpburger, where you'll be earning minimum wage for the rest of your miserable life by flipping burgers and cleaning the shitters. Are there any other questions? And I wasn't talking to you, lardass."

"I'd like to ask Tribianka a question if that's alright by you, Mr. President," implored a young girl with black hair and a ponytail who was sitting at the same table as the chubby kid. "Tribianka, you are the President's most senior advisor and one of the few women who work in the Crump administration. What I would like to know is what do you actually do at the Crump House? Also, what courses should I study in school, and how many years of experience would I need to qualify for a top job like yours in the US government?"

"Daddy said that I'm his favorite child and the only person in the world who could ever be his most senior advisor. I have a big office and lots of staff that do so many marvelous things. Or so Daddy always tells me. And I get to fly in Air Force One and meet all sorts of wonderful people like our friends, the Kims," giggled Tribianka, while holding Crump's hand.

"But what exactly does your job entail?" repeated the girl, who, after hearing Tribianka's answer, was none the wiser.

"Just a minute, Miss public school pain in the fukkin ass. All you need to know is that I have two winners on my team, and they're both worth their weight in gold. One is Tribianka Crump, and the other is my presidential intern from England, Trenton Begby, who is the young man standing over there. The rest of the fukkers that work for me are just a bunch of worthless lameass fuktards. At the Crump House, education and experience mean absolutely nothing. It's all about who you know and what you can do for me," blasted Crump, while shaking his head. "I'll take one more question before I leave, but kids, make sure it's not just shittossing fukdust this time."

"Mr. President, I'm Milton Poindexter, and I have a question for you," called out an older kid wearing glasses from the back of the gym. "I've been class president at Benedict Arnold Elementary for the past three years, and I have a 4.0 GPA and will be applying for early admittance to university in a couple of years. What I would like to know is which college did you attend, and for an overachiever like me, do you recommend MIT or a school from the Ivy League?"

"You've got to be shittin me, kid," laughed Crump, who turned his head towards me again and muttered, typical fukkin nerd. "Ivy League schools are for rich kids and not four-eyed penniless geeks like you, and the same goes for MIT. Let me tell you this for nothing, you don't get into the likes of Harvard or Yale with good grades. It takes a million-dollar bribe to gain admittance into those shitass schools. Take my fukbrained son-in-law, Waywerd. He never passed an exam in his entire asshole life, yet Harvard accepted him all the same after his old man slipped the shitmeister rowing coach and assbending Dean of Admissions a couple of million. I was much too clever to go to college myself and knew that no assclown could ever teach me anything I didn't already know. So I studied at the University of Life, and you can see where it got me. Of course, the best you can expect out of life is a supervisory position at Crumpburger, where you'll probably be managing that lardass over there."

"Thank you for your insightful words, Mr. President. I know that I speak for the entire faculty and student body when I say that it has been an honor and a privilege to have you as our guest at Benedict Arnold Elementary," trumpeted Principal Boggs, who was now standing at the front of the stage wearing an ASS cap and waving a Vote Crump pennant. "Before you leave us, do you have any departing words for our students?"

"Principal Boggs, as a matter of fact, I do. Kids, public school is for losers. If you want to get yourself out of the fukhouse, then you need to pay a shitload of cash for a private education. And the only way I can see any of you poor fukkers doing that is if you win the goddamn lottery or rob a fukkin bank," proclaimed Crump, as he yawned and gestured to Bich.

"Well, slap yo' Momma, Mr. President. Ya sure did tell them young'uns how it is," congratulated Bich, before calling OnYurway to escort the four kids who were to represent Benedict Arnold Elementary onto the stage.

While Crump and Tribianka were having their photos taken with the kids, I helped Bich and OnYurway register the rest of the student body as Republicans. Indoctrinating the kids as Crumpers at an early age had been one of Twatt Jabowsky's better ideas, and Crump, not surprisingly, had agreed. Needless to say, after looking down the barrel of one of OnYurway's magnums, dissenters were encouraged to register. And this meant that within the hour, we had successfully signed up every one of Benedict Arnold Elementary's young fukkers.

Once we were back in the sanitized comfort of the Beast, Crump ranted about how much he hated public schools and having to be exposed to the shitfilthy kids that attended them. Fortunately, on our return to the Crump House, the Surgeon General of the United States was waiting for Crump in the Oval Office. After examining the three of us for signs of infection, our contaminated clothing was sent to the incinerator, and, at that point, the nation's top doctor gave us the all-clear. Dressed in a presidential robe and slippers, Crump helped himself to a can of diet coke and handed another to me. Then, with Tribianka sitting on his lap, he turned on the television to SHITE news before saying we should call it a day.

The following morning, Crump's personal assistant informed me that after his hectic day at Benedict Arnold Elementary, Crump was having a well-earned lie-in. So not wanting to disturb the late riser, I ordered a Crumpburger before throwing caution to the wind by adding a cherry coke to my order at the drive-thru located on the North Lawn. Alone for once, I sat in the Rose Garden and devoured my greasy Crumpburger in no time at all. However, when it came to experiencing my very first cherry coke, I took one sip before feeding the foul-tasting beverage to the Crump House roses.

It was around one in the afternoon when I strolled into the Oval Office to find Crump at the Resolute desk practicing his arm wrestling technique with OnYurway. Meanwhile, Tribianka was sitting on the sofa with a vacant expression on her face and was painting her absurdly long nails a vibrant hot pink. And then there was Bich, who sat at the other end of the sofa noisily chowing down on a bucket of her Granny's chitlins smothered in apple cider vinegar and Louisiana hot sauce.

"Trenton, ya should try some of these here chitlins," called out Bich, who offered me the bucket filled with the Southern deep-fried delicacy. "These are not the regular kind with pig intestines. No, siree, these be Arkansas chitlins and are made from possums caught by my brother, Cooter. Ya know Granny's chitlins are the best in the county by far. That's because most other folks clean the intestines before they cook 'em, but Granny never does. She says why bother cleanin' the darn thin's when ya only goin' to shit 'em out later on."

"Thank you, Bich, but I've already eaten a Crumpburger, so I'm quite full." I politely informed the Crump House press secretary as I glanced at the stomach-churning fried snack she held in her hands.

"Well, if ya as full as a tick, then that means there's more for little ol' Bich," beamed Bich, as she crammed a handful of chitlins into her gaping hole of a mouth.

"Wise move, Trenton. Stick with Crumpburgers as all they contain is harmless fukkin mad cow. Only lamebrain Southerners and ASS men eat the sort of shit that Bich thrives on," laughed Crump, who had just won another arm wrestling bout against OnYurway. But only because, as usual, she had let her boss win. "Take a seat and help yourself to a can of diet coke. The Secretary of Education has an audience with me a little later, so it's going to be another busy day leading the pussyfooting free world."

By now, Crump had become bored of arm wrestling his senior counselor, so he decided to test his agility and speed by playing a few rounds of snap. The slow-witted Tribianka was chosen to be his opponent, and the Crump House press secretary would referee. After cheating his way through every game, Bich declared him the winner before Crump announced that it was time to take a break from his hectic workday to play a game of Twister.

Around three in the afternoon, just as the five of us fell onto the Twister mat giggling, there was a knock on the Oval Office door, and in walked Crump's Secretary of Education, Bitsy Dikshit. Like most of Crump's senior cabinet members, she was a barely literate high school drop-out with a wealth of moneyed connections. In the case of 27-year-old Bitsy, it was her octogenarian billionaire husband and Crump's long-time golfing partner, Elmer Dikshit. He was one of the Connecticut Dikshits who had donated a crapload of cash to the Crump campaign to get his highfaluting young wife a job in which she was woefully unqualified.

"Good afternoon, Mr. President. Hard at it, I see," chuckled Bitsy, as she parked herself on the sofa. "I hear that the fake press are none too impressed with the Crump Monument you're constructing. But what the hell, they're only shit poor peasants after all, so who gives a fuk."

"Granny always says that ya can please some of the fukkers all of the time, ya can please all of the fukkers some of the time, but ya can't please all of the fukkers all of the time. And if ya claim ya can, then ya got to be a goddamn pissass bullcrappin' hillbilly from Tennessee," chimed in Bich, who was untangling herself from OnYurway and Tribianka as she spoke.

"Why bother trying to please any of those chickenshit fukkers," shrugged Crump, as he walked over to the Resolute desk and sat down on his chair. "Bitsy, you're supposed to be my Secretary of Education, so I want to talk to you about fukkin public schools. Are you aware I visited that shitfilled Benedict Arnold Elementary yesterday afternoon with its asskissing principal, Homer Boggs?"

"I am, Mr. President. Elmer and I saw you on SHITE news last night, and we both thought you were absolutely fabulous. Although why you wanted to visit a public school is beyond me. I've never set foot in one myself. In fact, I've made it a rule to only go to functions held in private schools as their students come from a social class that's more in tune with my own," replied Bitsy, who was now lying on the sofa and receiving her daily Botox shots from Tribianka.

"That was Twatt Jabowsky's fukkin idea. He thinks that if

the goddamn voters are fooled into believing I actually support educating poor kids, then I'll gain a fukload of votes at the next election. I don't see it myself, but anyway, it got the old Crump grey matter thinking," explained Crump, as he rapped his knuckles on the side of his head. "I've already spoken to several Senate Republicans, and they agree with me when it comes to education. So, Bitsy, why the fuk are we throwing away shitloads of cash to educate good for nothing young fukkers when that money could just as easily go to me?"

"Mr. President, you're forgetting that we've already closed the cafeterias in every public school in the country and replaced them with Crumpburgers. So the only place the kids can spend their money during school hours is with you," responded Bitsy, somewhat defensively.

"I'm well aware that Crumpburger is making millions from the shitster public school system, but I didn't get to be a billionaire by accepting crumbs from the goddamn table. Not when I can have the whole fukkin pie," bawled Crump, as he slammed his fist down on the Resolute desk in a fit of rage.

"In England, school kids are given a test at the age of 11," I chimed in, with a can of diet coke in my hand. "If they pass, they can go to a good public school, which will allow them to get some qualifications to gain admittance to college and the chance of a first-rate job. But if they fail, they're sent to a shitty school to learn technical skills like how to bang a nail into a piece of wood."

"You know, I find socialist countries so quaint. However, in the land of the free, if you want to go to a good school, then you need to be rich enough to go private," laughed Bitsy, and then Tribianka joined in too. "And Trenton, in the capitalist US of A, all public schools are shitty, and I can assure you, that's just how the Founding Fathers wanted it."

"Bitsy, I believe that Trenton is on to something," interjected Crump, who had a smile on his face as he leaned back on his chair. "At least half of these degenerate public school kids are going to end up working in a Crumpburger, and the other half will undoubtedly go to fukkin prison. So why don't we teach them something useful like flipping burgers and cleaning shitters? We can rename the public schools and call them Crump Technical Schools, shitcan the current teaching staff, and use Crumpburger staff to train the young fukkers. That way, all the funding for these schools can go directly to me."

"I'm with you as always, Mr. President," answered Bitsy, as she applied a fresh coat of make-up to her flawless cosmetically enhanced face. "Although I'm not sure their wretched parents will like it, and that may influence who they vote for come Election Day. I've been told on good authority; the poor want their kids to do better in life and achieve more than they did. They're delusional, of course. What the fuk do they think this country is, the land of goddamn opportunity for losers or something? Then again, what can you expect from people that haven't gotten a private education like us."

"This is what you're going to do, Bitsy," commanded Crump, who was drinking his diet coke while signaling to Tribianka that he wanted her to sit on his lap. "The Department of Education will devise a national test to be taken by every five-year-old with parents who are too fukkin poor to pay the very reasonable fees charged by private schools. In the meantime, I'll make an announcement stating all those who pass will get a Crump scholarship to attend the private school of their choice. And the rest will go to a Crump Technical School that guarantees them a job at Crumpburger if they graduate. If that doesn't want to make the fukkers vote Crump, then they can go to hell."

"But, Mr. President, private schools are the exclusive domain of the rich. You can't seriously expect them to agree to this. The whole point of establishing the public education system in the first place was to separate people like us from society's chaff," argued Bitsy, with an alarmed expression on her face.

"What do you take me for, Bitsy, a shitcrazy Democrat?" scoffed Crump, as he turned on the television to watch SHITE news. "I'm not about to start handing out fukkin scholarships to anyone. They can take the goddamn test, but none of them will ever pass it. I shit you not, every last one of those young fukkers is going to a Crump Technical School whether they like it or not."

8

CRUMP on Health

"Exercise is a pissass waste of time and effort. Eat a Crumpburger instead!"
— Ronald S. Crump, President of the United States

* * *

The day after Crump met with Secretary Dikshit, Crump and I, along with Asyphilis, Tribianka, Bich, and OnYurway, flew down to the Caribbean for a short vacation at Kiss-my-Ass. After a week of golfing, tweeting shit, and doing sweet fuk-all while frolicking in the sun, we all boarded Air Force One. Although before we returned to the Crump House, the six of us attended a series of Crump re-election rallies in the heart of Crumper country organized by Twatt Jabowsky. These were held in the towns of Bugtussle – Kentucky, Mud Butte – South Dakota, Bumpass – Virginia, and Ding Dong – Texas, or as Twatt liked to say, the Real America.

"Trenton, I've decided to make a list of the names of every fukker I can think of that has aggrieved me. It's going to be a long list, and when I'm finished, I'll execute every goddamn one of them with that anti-aircraft gun sitting in the Rose Garden," remarked Crump, as we sat at the Resolute desk eating our lunch of Crumpburgers and diet coke the day after returning from Ding Dong. "I'm thinking of including the names of Twatt Jabowsky and the rest of the campaign team. They're all worthless fukwitted shitbaggers, so if I execute them, I won't need to pay their last month's salary or an assfukkin penny in severance. Come to think of it, if the executions take place on inauguration day, I'll be able to call it entertainment. And that'll mean the presidential inauguration fund will have to pay me a shitload of cash for hosting the fukkin thing."

"Howdy, y'all. It sure is a fine day out there. If I was still in Arkansas, I'd be out huntin' possums with Granny and Cooter on a day like this. Cooter is the best shot in the family, but as Granny likes to use an Uzi, she's the one who always comes home with the most possums," jabbered Bich, as she stormed into the Oval Office with Oleander OnYurway only a few steps behind her. "Mr. President, I've just been informed the Secretary of Health is comin' to see ya this afternoon about a crisis which could affect the health of the nation and the election. And the fukkers in the fake press have been assbadgerin' me about ya own health. They want to know whether ya are mentally and physically fit to lead the country for a third term."

"Bich, is this your lameass attempt at scratching my scrote?" barked Crump, who was pointing at the Crump House press secretary while giving her the fukeye. "I have a letter here that was written by me and signed by the Surgeon General of the United States stating I'm the healthiest president ever. And not only that, it says I have a mind that makes Einstein look like an assbrained dickbeating dumbfuk and a body of a fukkin 16-year-old."

"That's just hunky-dory, Mr. President. I'll use it in a Crump House press release once I'm finished here," nodded Bich, as she perused the piece of paper that Crump had handed her. "That'll stick it to those degenerate fukkers in the fake press who claim ya just a lazy senile old fukker who does nothin' but watch SHITE news and tweet shit all day."

"Trenton, no one is healthier than Crump. And you may not know this, but I pride myself on being the fittest person in the world," exclaimed Crump, while offering me another can of diet coke. "You probably think it's because I eat Crumpburgers every day. But between you and me, the real reason for my perfect health is that I never fukkin exercise. Trust me; you've got to be a shitheaded asswit to exercise. That's because everyone has a finite number of steps they can take in their life, which is why I rarely move. According to my calculations, at my current rate of inactivity, I'm going to outlast every fukker I know and live to the age of a goddamn 186."

As I jotted this down in my notepad, Crump practiced his arm wrestling with OnYurway, and Bich apprised us of the all-important goings-on outside of the Crump House. Conversions to Crumpism were going well, particularly amongst the Crumper evangelicals, which, presumedly, was on account of the free Crumpburger they received. And the dissolution of religious places of worship was moving along like a treat under the watchful eye and close supervision of Archbishop Dwight Jacoff. In their place, Crumpburgers, in the guise of the Church of Crump, were sprouting up in thousands of locations across the 49 states of the Union, much to Crump's merriment.

By the time Tribianka strolled into the Oval Office to play

snap with Crump, Bich had started to talk about the progress made in constructing the Crump Monument. Crump was clearly pleased that the foundations had been laid, and his pyramid to immortalize himself was finally taking shape. And he was delighted the monumental task of transporting huge blocks of North Korean granite to Washington, DC, was now underway. Accidents on the construction site were running at more than a dozen an hour, and there had been at least one fatality each day. Be that as it may, as there were plenty of undocumented immigrants sitting in detention centers around the country and more arriving at airports daily, the overseers from the Secret Service were confident the work would be finished by inauguration day.

In one of his many daily tweets, Crump announced the opening of Crump Technical Schools and the national test that every prospective public school kid would have to take. As he deemed free education beyond the age of 12 frivolous and unnecessary, as did the Republican Party leadership, Crump also decreed that public high schools were to be closed. This meant freeloading young fukkers wanting to further their education would now have to pay for it. Something private schools had been urging the GOP to enact for years. And in no small part to the millions in bribes paid to their members, the Grand Old Party readily agreed.

"So, Bich, how is this national test for those shitster five-year-olds coming along?" inquired Crump, just before he purposely distracted Tribianka. Then slammed a card down on the Resolute desk and yelled SNAP!

"Mr. President, comin' up with a test that five-year-olds are not goin' to be able to pass is like learnin' to milk a goddamn possum. Ya think it's goin' to be as easy as a Sunday school hog ride, right up to the moment ya get a mouthful of possum pee. That's when ya know, ya gonna have a real fukker of a time milkin' that darn possum," rambled Bich, who spoke as if the Arkansas ritual of milking possums was a common sight in the Crump House. "Secretary Dikshit thought her team had cracked it after none of the Crump House staff could pass the first fukkin test they devised. However, when they tested it out on a group of young'uns, every one of the badasses aced the mothafukka."

"Assmonkeys, the lot of them. I've got a mind to shitcan every fukker working in the Department of Education. And this time, I might hire people who can actually read and write for a change," snapped Crump, as he glared at Bich and threw his remaining cards on the table.

At that moment, there was a knock on the Oval Office door and in toddled Crump's Secretary of Health, Hank Krappa. A picture of health he definitely was not, as he must have weighed in at around a rotund 350lbs and could always be relied upon to be puffing on a cigarette. Naturally, the blusterous fellow had no qualifications to his name, except for a first-aid certificate from his years as health and safety manager at Crumpburger. This was a job that had only one function, which was to make it look like the health and safety of Crumpburger employees and customers was something Crump gave a shit about. Of course, if truth be told, the real reason that Crump created this position was to lower Crumpburger's insurance premium.

"Good afternoon, Mr. President. It's been a busy morning but a fukkin rewarding one, I can tell you," exclaimed Krappa, as he sat down on the sofa and put his feet on the coffee table. Then he placed his cigarette butt in an empty can of diet coke before lighting another of his favorite brand of cancer sticks. "You'll be pleased to know I've finally got that dicksneeze of a health warning removed from cigarette packs. As usual, the goddamn health-freak Surgeon General objected because he claimed cigarettes can kill you. Ha! What a jackass. Nevertheless, after I sat on him for an hour, the fukker soon came around to my way of thinking. This means free smokes for life for me and one hell of a sizeable donation from the tobacco lobby to the charity of your choice. If you get my drift."

"I do, Krappa. And good work. But why the fuk did you come down here and interrupt my hectic schedule? You could have told me this over the goddamn shitbreathing phone," grumbled Crump, who had folded his arms and was now giving the Secretary of Health the fukeye. "I thought you wanted to speak to me about another fukkin crisis, but it sounds like you're just giving me the fukaround and wasting my time."

"Oh yes, I nearly forgot about the goddamn health crisis. You know, that's the problem with having shit for brains, I can never remember any fukkin thing. Though I've found smoking helps, which is why I get through at least four packs a day," prattled Krappa, as he lit another cigarette from the dying embers of the one he had been smoking. "It's like this, Mr. President. For the past month, the Department of Health has been getting reports of a new and highly contagious ailment that reduces brain function and brings on madness. We think it may have started in Texas, only because that cowpoke with the big asshat, Governor Blink Calhoun, was the first to alert us. Although at the time, we thought nothing of it, because let's face it, you've got to be a crazy fukker to live in Texas in the first place."

"So, what of it, why should I give a shittossing flying fukeroo about some assbite of a malady in fukkin Texas of all places?" scoffed Crump, who was rolling his eyes with his arms outstretched and the palms of his hands facing the ceiling.

"You're right, Mr. President. If it was just Texas, then obviously, the Department of Health wouldn't give a shit. Let's face it, that godforsaken hellhole only became a US state because in the 1800s a rowdy bunch of pissassin fukboys stole it from Mexico," replied Krappa, in-between coughs and puffing on his cigarette. "The reason I brought this to you now is that it's spreading unchecked throughout the Southern States and the fukkin Midwest."

"Krappa, you do know that you're talking about Crumper country. And the fukkers that live in those shitass states are not only the ones who vote Crump, but they're also Crumpburger's best customers. This sounds like Democrat fukery and a blatant fukkin attempt to deny me my destiny as president for life," fumed Crump, as he slammed his fist down on the Resolute desk. "Bich, I want you to send out a press release stating Smilin' Mo Fudrucker and LSD are trying to steal this election from me. And you can also say that my personal attorney, Shifty Daniels, has a crapload of evidence proving the goddamn left-wing deep state is behind this."

"I wouldn't do that if I were you, Mr. President," interjected Krappa, just as Crump was frantically typing one of his famously inflammatory falsehood-ridden tweets.

"And why the assfuk is that?" demanded Crump, as he glowered at the Secretary of Health.

"Oh, didn't I tell you? There you go again, shit for brains, just like everyone in our family. Anyhow, a couple of weeks ago, I sent a crack unit of Navy SEALs down to Texas to capture some of the infected fukkers. Most of them didn't return, but the three who did were able to bring back a live one," explained Krappa, who was now kicking off his shoes while lighting another cigarette. "I had our science division give him the once-over, and they believe he's contracted a new form of mad cow disease that only affects humans. The experts tell me it's highly contagious, but who's to know. They're calling it BSE–T487Z, which is a fukkin stupid name if you ask me. That's why for the past week, I've been in the Bahamas holed up in a 5-star megaresort with my best people, brainstorming a better one. So the Department of Health is now calling it Mad Fukker Disorder or MFD for short."

"Daddy, can I see the mad fukker, can I?" squealed Tribianka, as she walked over to the Resolute desk and sat on Crump's lap.

"I'm not so sure about that, dear. I wouldn't want my little girl and most senior advisor to catch this disease and turn into a mad fukker. Don't forget, I already have a fukload of them working for me in the Crump House," answered Crump, while pointing his finger at Bich. "Besides, I'm sure this mad fukker they captured is safely locked away in a maximum-security facility a long, long way from here. Isn't that right, Krappa?"

"No, as a matter of fact, he's with us here in the West Wing," revealed Krappa, who was crushing his now empty cigarette pack and opening a new one. "I've got him chained to the wall in the stationary closet at the back of my office. It's been a real fukkin hoot, I can tell you. I'm charging $25 a pop to feed the mad fukker a Crumpburger and the same to have a selfie taken with him. But don't worry, Mr. President. Even though the stationary closet door has no lock, he won't be getting out of there in a hurry because I've wedged a chair under the doorknob."

"Krappa, you goddamn dickstick, I thought you said this mad fukker is highly contagious," yelled Crump, as he threw an empty can of diet coke at his Secretary of Health. "If you've exposed me, Tribianka, and Trenton to this Mad Fukker Disorder, then I'm going to have OnYurway shoot you in that fukdust head of yours with one of her magnums."

"Give me some credit, Mr. President," laughed Krappa, while lighting yet another cigarette. "You have to be bitten by a mad fukker to contract MFD. And they don't just stroll up and bite you out of the blue. No, Sir, they always moo first before trying to bite you. In the beginning, the Navy SEALs who went down to Texas thought mooing was some kind of assclown Texan greeting, which is why so many of them were bitten. Unfortunately, the three SEALs that made it back unscathed are pretty cut up because they had to shoot their fallen comrades in the head. Though as far as I can understand, there was no medical reason to do this. Nevertheless, all three told me they had seen it done that way on the television, so it seemed like a good idea to them at the time."

"Secretary Krappa, do you have any idea how humans became infected with this new form of mad cow disease in the first place?" I asked, as I was eager to learn more about the origins of Mad Fukker Disorder,

"That's an asskicker of a question, Trenton," acknowledged Crump, who turned to me and nodded his approval. "Krappa, while you and the other dickweasels at the Department of Health were in the fukkin Bahamas, did anyone bother doing any shitdigging to find out where Mad Fukker Disorder came from?"

"Mr. President, not everyone at the Department of Health sits on their asses all day playing cards and shooting the fukkin breeze. Admittedly, most of us do, but we've also got a few kissass geeks in the office to do the lion's share of the work," reassured Krappa, while blowing smoke rings in my direction.

"According to our top mad cow expert, Doctor, whatever the fuk his name is, it's something to do with the high concentration of BSE in Crumpburgers."

"Nonsense, Krappa, I've been eating Crumpburgers all my life, and you don't see me going around mooing and biting every fukker I come across," retorted Crump, and Tribianka nodded her ditzy head in agreement.

"I won't give you a brainfuk by talking scientific shit, Mr. President, because I don't understand a cockbite of it myself," confessed Krappa, as he stubbed out his cigarette and lit a new one. "What I can tell you is that eating two or three Crumpburgers a day poses little harm to anyone. However, if you eat a shitload of them over a prolonged period, there's a chance your brain will get what the doctors like to term, a BSE overload, and that can really fuk you up. That's why Texas is ground zero for MFD. The fukkers down there eat Crumpburgers by the bucketful, and that's how some of them turned into mad fukkers and started biting people. The Republican governors have already deployed National Guard units in the affected states. But as most mad fukkers are heavily armed ASS men, the firepower is shitstacked against them. We can put a warning on every Crumpburger that eating too many may be detrimental to your health. Though, when it comes to stopping the current spread of MFD, someone needs to find a cure before it's too late and the country becomes inundated with mad fukkers."

"So Krappa, you're telling me some goddamn Crumpers in Texas caught Mad Fukker Disorder by eating my Crumpburgers. They then began mooing before biting their fellow Crumpers. Who in turn became mad fukkers themselves," restated Crump, while shaking his head and rolling his eyes.

"That's pretty much it, Mr. President," nodded Krappa, with

a sigh. "Also, the ASS men amongst them like to shoot their guns in the air as well, but I suppose that's nothing out of the ordinary for Dic Hade's ASS capped fukkers."

"Krappa, there's no fukkin way I'm going to authorize warning signs on Crumpburgers. I'd have to be a mad fukker myself to do something asscrazy like that," growled Crump, as he reached for a can of diet coke. "How long will it take for the Department of Health to develop a cure because this could really eat into Crumpburger sales? And do you know whether these mad fukkers are capable of voting for me at the next election?"

"Well, Mr. President, finding a cure to a highly contagious disease entails solving an assload of problems. Unfortunately, the US Department of Health is a disorganized fukhole and shitawful at solving problems. In actual fact, we're usually the ones who create them. So, if you're relying on us to come up with the cure to MFD, I wouldn't hold out much hope if I were you," declared Krappa, with a chuckle. "And in my opinion, when it comes to voting, there's no reason why a mad fukker won't vote Crump. If India is to go by, you may even increase your fukkin share of the vote."

"What has India got to do with mad fukkers, Krappa?" yelled Crump, who by now was losing his patience with the dimwitted Secretary of Health. "Most of the fukkers living in that fukkin country don't even eat Crumpburgers, so they can't have an outbreak of Mad Fukker Disorder there too."

"I know, Mr. President, as far as I'm aware, there are no reported cases of MFD in India, not yet anyway. But don't forget, their government supplies Crumpburger with a fukass load of mad cows every year," disclosed Krappa, while reaching for a can of diet coke and another cigarette. "And though they don't eat BSE infected beef like us enlightened Americans, they do drink mad cow pee like it's fukkin water. It was their wacko prime minister who first got them hooked on it when he came to power years ago. And now he has a whole country of crazy fukkers that always vote for him no matter what chicken-assed policies he and the shitgreasers in his party come up with."

"Krappa, we don't need every voter to turn into a mad fukker for me to beat Smilin' Mo Fudrucker. There are enough fukkin Crumpers in this country to guarantee me victory. And as long as Crumpers with Mad Fukker Disorder vote Crump, then that's alright by me," uttered Crump, as Tribianka retreated to the sofa to allow her father to tweet. "The real shitdinger to this is that Crumpburger sales may suffer, so I'm going to declare a national emergency and order the US Army into the affected states. They can keep these mad fukkers at bay, and in the meantime, I want you to form a task force with a bunch of top asskicking doctors and scientists to find a cure. I'll put that asswipe, Mylo Peckerhead, in charge. That way, I can use him as a scapegoat if the shit hits the fan, which it invariably does at the Crump House. And Krappa, you can haul that sorry ass of yours back to your nutsack of an office now, and don't forget to take every one of those fukkin cigarette butts with you."

Once Secretary Krappa had left, at Crump's request, I opened a window in the room to let in some fresh air. And, needless to say, allow the lingering foul-smelling stench of cigarette ash to ebb away. Then, while listening to Crump fume about the impact of MFD on Crumpburger sales, the five of us were startled by the deafening Crump House sirens. As usual, all hell broke loose as Secret Service agents ran into the Oval Office, locked and barricaded the door, then formed a defensive perimeter with their weapons drawn.

As this was an all too common occurrence at the Crump

House, Crump rolled his eyes and yawned. And then, after the din of the sirens died down, he helped himself to a can of diet coke before casually turning on the television to watch SHITE news. Although seconds later, things abruptly took a turn for the worse when we heard the distinctive clamor of an overweight individual running down the corridor on the other side of the Oval Office door. Hearing the gasping breathless wheeze of a heavy smoker, which could only have come from the lungs of Secretary Krappa, Crump muted the television, and the room went silent.

The next thing we heard was a bone-chilling scream, and the ominous words, "Mad fukker," were expelled from the mouth of the Secretary of Health like a bat out of hell. Then as I glanced at Crump, and he looked back at me, the sound of a mad fukker's moo could clearly be discerned. As the Secret Service was sworn to protect Crump and no one else, no matter how hard Hank Krappa yelled, "I've been fukkin bitten," and repeatedly banged his fists on the door, the sturdy Oval Office door remained closed.

A minute or two passed by, and then another moo could be heard, followed by the sound of a tricycle and a voice calling out, "I'm going to the moo-oon too."

After I saw Crump shake his head while muttering the words, "Fukkin moron," he clicked his fingers to get the attention of his senior counselor. And then, with a flick of the wrist, he drew a finger across his throat before ordering the Secret Service to dismantle the barricade and unlock the door. The moment the door was flung open, the distraught Secretary Krappa staggered in. But alas for the poor fellow, OnYurway coolly pulled out one of her magnums and shot him in the head.

With the Secretary of Health now stone dead, Crump's senior

counselor stepped into the corridor and gunned down the mad fukker too. Then seeing that Birk had been bitten as well and would likely be next on OnYurway's hit list, I implored Crump to spare his youngest son's life. And though Crump was reluctant at first, he finally agreed after I convinced him that a living, breathing mad fukker would be needed if a cure for MFD was to be found.

In the days following that fateful afternoon in the Crump House, the MFD task force had been convened posthaste with Crump's Vice President as its head. A top team of doctors and scientists were brought in to work on a cure, which meant Birk was now the subject of round-the-clock experiments. As Crump did not want it known a member of the Crump family had been bitten by a mad fukker, blabbing to the press was made a treasonable offense. And to ensure he could not bite anyone important, once he turned into a mad fukker himself, Birk currently resided in a dungeon beneath the newly rebuilt East Wing.

Over the coming weeks, to Crump's annoyance, mad fukkers multiplied at an alarming rate, most notably in Crumper states. As he feared, this was a devastating blow to Crumpburger's top-line revenue as every Crumper who turned into a mad fukker meant fewer Crumpburgers would be eaten. Crump's tweets denying the existence of MFD and his claim that there was no such thing as a mad fukker, only patriotic ASS men and loyal Crumpers blowing off a little steam, were routinely derided by the scientific community. And although this made Crump fume, what irritated him the most was the skeptical fake press talking about the growing number of mad fukkers. Not to mention the daily count of new MFD infections in each state.

"Howdy, Mr. President. Those fukkers in the fake press are

now callin' it a goddamn pandemic that has been mismanaged from the outset," announced Bich, as she and OnYurway marched into the Oval Office one afternoon. "And they say at this fukkin rate the whole shitass country will be overrun with mad fukkers by year's end."

"As President of the US of A, I take credit for every fukkin thing, but I'm not going to be held responsible for anything. If the shitshovelers in the fake press want to point their finger at someone, then make sure it's directed at that dick-for-brains, Mylo Peckerhead," hissed Crump, who was somewhat irked by his press secretary interrupting our game of snap. "Bich, tell Peckerhead I want to see the number of mad fukkers drop by the end of the week. I've already agreed to give Texas back to Mexico for a fukload of cash, so that should help. And if we accelerate global warming, that'll rid us of all those mad fukkers in Florida."

"No need for that, Mr. President. Ya can tell him ya'self soon enough because the Vice President is on his way to the Oval Office as we speak. He's got some important news for ya that just can't wait," pointed out Bich, while chowing down on a large bag of greasy deep-fried chili crawfish she was holding in her hand. "Ya know, I'm just plum worn slap out talkin' about mad fukkers, and I have another shitwaggin' press briefin' later this afternoon. We're gettin' reports that cases of Mad Fukker Disorder are poppin' up all over the globe. And some of the so-called fukkin experts on the MFD task force claim it's only a matter of time before mad fukkers become the dominant species on the planet. Oh well, Granny likes to say that whatever goes around always comes back to bite ya on the ass. But what do I know, I'm just a redneck from Arkansas, so as long as they don't take my guns away, I really don't give a shit."

"If SHITE news continues to be the number one news channel in America, and the SHITE buddies keep shitwagging everything we feed them, then their dickbrained viewers will vote Crump. And believe me, that's all that matters," asserted Crump, with an artful-looking grin. "Bich, what's the latest on Birk? I hope you've reminded the guards in the dungeon that if so much as a solitary moo comes out of that fukker's mouth, they shouldn't hesitate to shoot him in the fukkin head."

"Well, I've not seen Birk myself, but Tribianka has visited him in the dungeon almost every day. As ya well know, Mr. President, I come from a big family in Arkansas with more brothers and pappies to my young'uns than I care to remember. So it's heartenin' to see how devoted a sister can be to the wellbein' of a younger brother," answered Bich, after polishing off her last crawfish and licking her fingers clean. "She tells me that Birk hasn't turned into a mad fukker yet, although no one knows the fuk why. All the same, she spends two or three hours a day proddin' him with that 100,000 volt shock-stick of hers and chasin' the little tyke around his cell. If nothin' else, it gives him some exercise because they have him chained to the wall of the dungeon for the rest of the day."

"That's just typical of the asshead. From the minute Birk was born, he was always slow at everything, which is why I put him in charge of NASA," chided Crump, as he shook his head in disapproval. "It's been a month since he was bitten, and he's still the same dumbass Birk. If the dickstain was worth anything, he would have turned into a mad fukker by now."

"Exciting news, Mr. President," called out Mylo Peckerhead, who had entered the Oval Office unnoticed and was now walking towards the Resolute desk, waving a piece of paper in his hand. "We've done it! The MFD task force has discovered a cure for

Mad Fukker Disorder."

"It's about fukkin time," snapped Crump, as he opened a can of diet coke and leaned back on his chair. "So that means you can finally put me out of my misery by euthanizing Birk."

"I'm afraid not, Mr. President. Birk is the cure, which makes him humanity's only hope if we are to rid the world of this terrible affliction," blurted Mylo, as he handed the piece of paper to Crump, who immediately passed it to me without reading a word. "The doctors believe the reason Birk has not turned into a mad fukker after all these weeks is that he is immune to the effects of MFD. And that means we can use him to produce a vaccine to prevent the rest of us turning into mad fukkers ourselves."

"Humanity's only fukkin hope! Mylo, you call this good news? It was only two years ago that the fukhead realized he had to lift the lid before using the shitter. And he still thinks the bidet in the presidential bathroom is a water fountain," rebuked Crump, while giving his Vice President the fukeye. "Trenton, what does it say in that jerkoff piece of paper you're holding?"

"It looks like the task force doctors carried out a series of rigorous tests on Birk's brain. And then they compared the results with brain scans from several captured mad fukkers," I explained, as best I could. "What they found was that Birk's brain functions at a decidedly lower level than the brain of a mad fukker, and that's why he never contracted Mad Fukker Disorder after being bitten. By harvesting his brain cells, they believe a vaccine can be developed in no time at all, which should protect most people from becoming infected. Regrettably, though, those unlucky enough to have already contracted MFD will most likely continue to be mad fukkers for the rest of their natural lives."

"Trenton, the reason I'm so goddamn rich is that I can smell a good business opportunity a fukkin mile away," laughed Crump, with a gleam in his eyes. "You may not be aware of this, but I own Birk, and I have a bill of sale to prove it. In fact, I own all my children and grandchildren, and I even own Asyphilis. I had Shifty Daniels set it up that way because if ever any of them were to make a success of something, however unlikely that may be, I would own it. And that means yours truly owns the rights to any vaccine developed using the cells from Birk's fukker of a brain."

"But, Crump, what's to become of the people who have already turned into mad fukkers?" I asked, out of genuine concern. "Don't forget that most of them are gun-toting ASS men, and not only that, their Crumpers to boot. Surely you can't let them wander aimlessly from town to town, causing a nuisance to all and sundry by firing their guns and biting folk."

"Um, Trenton, you've got a point. I'll have the General round up as many mad fukkers as he and his boys can get their hands on. Then I'll tweet a decree to release every convict housed in state penitentiaries and call it prison reform. That should keep some of those twatlipped Botox-laden Hollywood types happy, and at the same time win me some goddamn votes. The empty prisons can house all these mad fukkers, and when it comes time to vote, they can make their mark on the ballot paper for Crump," proclaimed Crump, as he nodded his head as if to say to me, fukkin well-done. "And Mylo, I want you to ensure those scientists on the MFD task force have this vaccine ready within the week. In the meantime, I'll have every scrotelicking pharmaceutical company CEO on the planet sign a licensing deal to manufacture the vaccine and give me 60% of the profits. That way, there should be a shitload of cash coming my way by the end of the year."

"Of course, Mr. President," confirmed Mylo, while instinctively nodding his head. "However, it typically takes a series of lengthy trials over many years to test the efficacy of a vaccine and for the FDA to certify it safe for humans."

"Mylo, you shitbrained asslicker, you're missing the goddamn point as usual. I don't give a shit about the dickswingers in the FDA or whether the vaccine is safe or not. This is all about the money I'm going to be making. Besides, what's the worst that can happen with an untested vaccine? I'll tell you, a few worthless fukkers end up like Birk. So what, it's no big deal because there's plenty more where they came from," bellowed Crump, as he pointed his finger in a threatening manner at the Vice President. "You know what, I'm going to name this vaccine, Crump, and everyone in the world will have to pay to get a shot of Crump or else risk turning into a mad fukker. Now, Bich, you mentioned something about a fukkin press briefing this afternoon. You'll be pleased to know that Trenton and I will be coming along too."

9

CRUMP on Climate Change

"If you can't take the heat, then you should go and live in fukkin Alaska!"
— Ronald S. Crump, President of the United States

* * *

Upon entering the Fukkers Briefing Room, a rather loud and altogether unexpected moo rang out, followed by Vaj Ingersol of the SHITE buddies screeching, "Mad fukker!" Frantic screams were then heard coming from the mouth of the Washington Ghost reporter, Dillard Wowser. Meanwhile, two Secret Service agents pushed Crump to the floor, and the rest pulled out their guns and surrounded the indignant president. Then, during the split second that Oleander OnYurway fired her magnums into the air, members of the Crump House press corps dived for cover.

"Do me a favor. It was only a fukkin joke," called out Loudmouth Lonnie Laverty, who had his hands raised above his head as he crouched on the floor.

"Loudmouth, are ya bitchassin me?" yelled Bich, as she stood at the podium pointing her Arkansas toothpick at the SBC reporter. "Ya goddamn shitwagger, ya just earned ya'self three months in the misbehavin' fukkers section. So haul ya jerkoff ass to the back of the room, and if ya get up to any more fukery, then ya gonna be reacquainted with OnYurway and her magnums. And Wowser, ya pussyfootin' dickstick, if I hear another dickass scream come out of ya fukkin mouth, ya gonna be joinin' Loudmouth."

After the ruffled Crump was helped to his feet, he pulled up a chair next to mine, and into my ear, he simply muttered, "Fukkers." Then once the Crump House press corps was seated again and OnYurway had escorted Loudmouth Lonnie Laverty to the misbehaving fukkers section, Bich opened the briefing. She began by praising the SHITE buddies on their fair and unbiased fact-based coverage of the pandemic. Not unexpectedly, they had blamed the democrats for everything and claimed Smilin' Mo Fudrucker and LSD were both mad fukkers themselves and therefore unfit to hold public office. A beaming Vaj Ingersol then stood up and congratulated Crump on his outstanding leadership during the pandemic and stressed Mad Fukker Disorder was no fault of his. At which point, the Crump House press secretary stepped aside to allow Crump to take his place at the podium.

"Crump, so you're now admitting there is a pandemic after denying the existence of mad fukkers for the past month," shouted Loudmouth Lonnie Laverty, only moments before being pistol-whipped by OnYurway.

"That's goddamn fake news, and you know it. I deny that I've ever denied any such fukkin thing," raged Crump, as he watched OnYurway drag the now unconscious reporter from the

141

room. "If it wasn't for my exemplary leadership, there'd be no cure for Mad Fukker Disorder. And all you ungrateful assclowns would turn into a herd of mooing mad fukkers yourselves."

"Mr. President, do you mean to say that the MFD task force led by Mylo Peckerhead has developed a cure for Mad Fukker Disorder?" asked Raz Alvarez of DNN, in a somewhat mistrustful tone of voice. "And if that is indeed true, why isn't he standing at the podium to announce this breakthrough himself and answer questions?"

"Raz, I don't mind telling you and the other fukkers who represent the fake press that it's 100% true. We'll have a vaccine ready by the end of the week, and I can assure you that it's going into mass production soon after. And for your information, Mylo Peckerhead is the fukkin Vice President and not the President. That means I take all the credit myself and not Peckerhead or any of the shitdiggers on the MFD task force," ranted Crump, who turned to give me a thumbs-up before continuing. "You know, I deserve the Nobel Prize for Medicine for this, and probably a whole bunch of other prizes and medals for saving every fukker on the planet."

"All hail Crump!" cried out Vaj Ingersol, and then, while the rest of the Crump House press corps remained seated, she gave Crump a solitary standing ovation. "Congratulations, Mr. President. Everyone across the globe will be forever grateful the leader of the free world is Ronald S. Crump. And I, for one, will be nominating you for every Nobel Prize going."

"Thank you, Vaj. I'm calling the MFD vaccine, Crump. And as essential frontline workers, you and your fellow SHITE buddies will be first in line to get a shot of Crump," nodded Crump, while giving the SHITE buddy a wink. "And I want all you fukkers in the fake press to know that I've sacrificed a lot to bring this vaccine to fruition. In fact, without my youngest son, Birk, whose body I selflessly gave to science, there would be no cure to Mad Fukker Disorder."

"Mr. President, does this mean that Birk Crump, the head of NASA, is dead?" inquired Raz Alvarez, who was standing with her hand held high in the air. "And is this the reason you called the MFD vaccine, Crump, in honor of Birk?"

"Dead! Chance would be a fine thing. That fukker has got more lives than a nagass cat," retorted Crump, with a sigh and a shake of the head. "And Raz, the fukkin MFD vaccine is named after me because I'm the goddamn president."

"Mr. President, will you be awarding Birk the Presidential Medal of Freedom for his contribution to saving humanity?" blurted Dillard Wowser, while energetically waving his hands in the air to get Crump's attention.

"Wowser, do I look like a lamebrained cockbite to you? Of course, I'm not giving Birk the Presidential Medal of Freedom. You'll be asking me to award Hank Krappa one next, and all that useless lardass ever did was get himself bitten by a mad fukker. But now you've brought the subject up, I think I'll give it to someone more deserving, like myself. And while I'm about it, I should get the Congressional Medal of Honor and the fukkin Congressional Gold Medal as well," barked Crump, who signaled to me to jot this down in my notepad.

"Crump, is this vaccine going to be made available to every member of the public for free?" hollered Jem Tossa of NBS, from the back of the room in the misbehaving fukkers section.

"Of course not, Tossa, you fukheaded dickwit," bellowed Crump, and then he turned to me and rolled his eyes.

"I thought so," muttered Jem Tossa, before raising his voice again to ask Crump another question. "So what happens to people who can't afford your fukkin vaccine?"

"Tossa, I'm the leader of the free world, and so I really don't give a shit. If those dicksneezes want a shot of Crump, then they'll need to pay for each and every one of them. Failing that, they'll just have to drink bleach," replied Crump, with a chuckle.

"Oh, does bleach protect you from turning into a mad fukker too?" chimed in Dillard Wowser, who was widely known in the Crump House press corps for being exceedingly gullible and a little slow on the uptake.

"No, it doesn't, you dickfuk. It'll probably kill you," laughed Crump, before giving me another thumbs-up.

"Mr. President, I'm glad to hear that we now have a vaccine for Mad Fukker Disorder, which hopefully will put an end to this harrowing pandemic. I would now like to ask you about a far greater menace facing this country, indeed the world. And that is climate change," implored Mallory Hightower of CPR, who was sitting on a seat in the first row, directly in front of the podium.

"Not global fukkin warming again! Mallory, are you a fukaholic, or just a doddering old cumbubble?" snapped Crump, while pointing his finger at the venerable CPR reporter. "I have it on good authority from the experts in the coal, oil, and gas lobby that it's simply bullcrap concocted by the shittossers in the left-wing deep state. That's why they bankrolled my first election campaign with the condition I close down the asscrazy Environmental Protection Agency once I'm elected president. And as you well know, I did just that on my second day in office."

"Yes, Mr. President, everyone in the Crump House press corps knows that you are a brazen climate change denier, and we are all too aware of your administration's unscientific environmental policies," quipped Mallory Hightower, before receiving an enthusiastic hear-hear from her colleagues in the fake press. "The fact of the matter is that the world's air quality is declining, sea levels are rising, and hurricanes and tornadoes have been increasing in both frequency and severity. So on behalf of my CPR listeners, with the global apocalypse looming, are you going to do something about it, or just sit on your fat ass in the Oval Office, as usual? And will you be attending the global climate change summit for world leaders that is to be held next week?"

"Mallory, before I reply to your assdinger questions, I'd just like to say, fuk you!" scoffed Crump, while giving her the middle finger. Then Crump called over to me to add Mallory Hightower's name to the list of fukkers that have aggrieved him. "Now, with regards to your first question, I really don't give a goddamn fukeroo about global warming. Even if it was true, so what, I'm all in favor of getting a fukkin tan. And don't you know that I not only have a shitass country to run but Crumpburger as well? So why would I travel to the middle of nowhere to waste my valuable time attending a dreary jerkoff summit for assholes? Out of interest, which godforsaken shithole country is hosting the fukker this time?"

"That'd be this one, Mr. President. It's goin' to be held in Las Vegas," called out Bich, who was sitting at the back of the stage licking redneck caviar from her fingers.

"Vegas!" repeated Crump, as he turned his head and glared at Bich. "Right, this fukkin briefing is over. Come with me, Trenton. And Bich, I want to see your Arkansas ass in the Oval Office in five minutes."

Back in the Oval Office, Crump ranted and fumed while I opened a couple of cans of diet coke, one for him and the other for me. Although I had not yet visited the undisputed cultural heart of America myself, it was quite evident that Crump had been to the celebrated entertainment mecca many times before. Almost 20 minutes went by before there was a feeble knock on the door, and in walked a grinning Bich Landers, followed, as usual, by the magnum toting Oleander OnYurway.

"Why didn't you tell me about this fukkin climate change summit that's taking place in Las Vegas?" thundered Crump, and then he threw the empty can he was holding in his hand at the Crump House press secretary.

"Hold your horses, Mr. President, I was fixin' to, but then I just plum fukkin forgot," confessed Bich, with a shrug of the shoulders. "Anyhows, ya told me to leave global warmin' to the fukkers in the Democratic Party. And besides, the others are goin'. So ya don't need to worry ya big ol' ass about this good for nothin' summit."

"Bich, I don't give a shit about the summit. But if it's to be held in Vegas, I can assure you, I'll be there," snarled Crump, as he gave his press secretary the fukeye. "And when you say the others will be going, what the assfuk do you mean?"

"Well, Mr. President, accordin' to ya personal assistant, except for Bitsy Dikshit, the entire cabinet will be attendin'. Though, of course, Hank Krappa had to drop out on account OnYurway shot him dead after he was bitten by that goddamn mad fukker," explained Bich, while nodding her head. "Oh yes, and the Vice President will be there as well to deliver a keynote address to the other world leaders."

"What, a keynote fukkin address! The only reason that holier-than-thou evangelical fukker is going to Vegas is the whole asskicking town is brimming with dickslapping hookers," sneered Crump, as he opened another can of diet coke. "Bich,

146

Peckerhead is staying put right here, and I'm going to Vegas with Trenton, and I suppose you and OnYurway will have to come along too. I'll deliver the shittossing keynote address, and while I'm gone, Dwight Jacoff can convert fukkin Peckerhead to Crumpism. And those other lazy good-for-nothing fukkers aren't going anywhere either because I'm having another cabinet reshuffle. So I want you to tell that shitheaded personal assistant of mime to book us into my favorite hotel. And once she's done that, you can shitcan her worthless ass and hire another one."

Over the next few days, I looked forward to my trip to Las Vegas with Crump and learned a thing or two about cabinet reshuffles in the Crump House. The vacant Secretary of Health position, previously held by the late Hank Krappa, was purchased by the recently unemployed Governor of Texas, Blink Calhoun. And then, because it was all a game to Crump, he made the other cabinet members play musical chairs. This way, he could watch the fukkers squirm as none of them knew which cabinet position they would get or who was going to be shitcanned, and, needless to say, that included Crump.

Seeing that bringing female companions to Las Vegas was frowned upon, Tribianka stayed behind with Waywerd Pushover and their horde of kids, while Asyphilis flew down to Kiss-my-Ass for a week in the sun. This allowed Crump the opportunity to make a few extra bucks on the side by renting out the Executive Residence on Airbnb. And to Crump's glee, he did this in no time at all to a rowdy but likable bunch of vodka-swilling fellows from Russian Intelligence.

"Trenton, I love Vegas, and it's not just because of the whoring and gambling and all-out debauchery. Though, I admit, that's pretty fukkin enticing," remarked Crump, as we flew to Nevada aboard Air Force One. "No, what I like about Las Vegas is that it's got everything worth seeing in the world without having to step foot in the shithole countries where they're to be found. You can visit Venice and not have to meet any goddamn arm-waving Italians, and Paris, which is thankfully bereft of the dickwad garlic-reeking French. And it's even got the best of Hollywood, but with none of those shitbreathing liberal fukkers from California trying to stick their heads up your ass."

The second we touched down at McCarran International Airport in Las Vegas, I could see the boyish excitement in Crump's eyes. Then as Air Force One taxied down the runway to the executive terminal, Crump handed me a Crumpburger cap and a t-shirt emblazoned with the words, What Goes Down in Vegas, Stays in Fukkin Vegas! As I removed my formal shirt and tie and replaced them with the t-shirt, Crump did the same before we both pulled on our Crumpburger caps.

Not surprisingly, Crump was the first to deplane, but I was hot on his heels, and Bich and OnYurway were not far behind. As Nevada was one of those inane states which allowed its residents to arm themselves with as many guns and as much ammunition as one could carry, ASS men were commonplace. This meant 300 heavily armed Secret Service agents had to be deployed in Las Vegas to safeguard Crump during our weeklong stay. And not only that, but the presidential motorcade was to be protected by a 1,000 strong force from the US Marine Corps along with a bunch of badass fukkers from Delta Force, a dozen Bradley Fighting Vehicles, and no less than six M1 Abrams tanks.

The presidential motorcade was certainly a sight to behold as we trundled up Las Vegas Boulevard flanked by the eagle-eyed Marines with their M16s to the ready. In case we came across a roadside bomb, Bich and OnYurway were placed in the lead car, while Crump and I sat in the Beast drinking diet coke. And, as one might expect, there was an M1 Abrams tank to our front and rear. As we entered The Strip, Crump opened the moonroof of the Beast, and then we both stood on the backseat, wolf-whistling and waving our arms in the air. At which point, remembering the best buffet in town for under 20 bucks was close by, Crump directed the motorcade to make a detour.

After Delta Force had forcibly cleared the restaurant and ruffed up several of its customers in the process, Crump, Bich, OnYurway, and I strapped on our feedbags. Then with Bich taking the lead, we delved into the delights of a Las Vegas all-you-can-eat buffet to gorge ourselves senseless. During the next hour, along with many other delicacies, we ate plate after plate of King crab legs until the buffet manager informed us we had eaten their entire day's supply. Dissatisfied with the restaurant's level of service, Crump raged and then launched into a profanity-laced outburst before refusing to pay. And that's when OnYurway fired her magnums into the air as we stormed out of the restaurant to the waiting presidential motorcade.

Upon our arrival at the Playboy Hotel, Crump and I were swiftly ushered to the presidential penthouse suite, while Bich and OnYurway checked into their rooms on the floor below. Then, after finishing an award-winning porn movie starring a former acquaintance of Crump's and drinking several cans of diet coke, it was time to hit a casino or two. But before I could enter the first of the many gambling dens we were to frequent that week, as a rite of passage, Crump insisted we head over to the Eiffel Tower first.

"Trenton, this is the life. Now, I hope everyone has drunk enough diet coke because on my command, we're all going to wazz together," exclaimed Crump, as we leaned over the railing on the top floor of the Eiffel Tower with six Secret Service agents by our side. Then, with all eight of us waving our arms in the air, Crump shouted go, and we wazzed onto the fukkers below. "Did we hit Bich and OnYurway?"

"I think so," I replied, while peering down on the Las Vegas Strip. "They were standing directly beneath us and looking up, just like you told them too."

"That's a hoot. They're total fukjobs, the both of them. Trenton, this is what real presidential power is all about. You know, if I click my fingers, the fukkers do absolutely anything I say. Just like these dumbasses in the Secret Service who would jump right now if I ordered them too," laughed Crump, just as we were zipping up our pants and walking to the elevator. "And don't forget that this week is on the goddamn US taxpayer. We can expense fukkin everything, and that includes the hookers. And if we win on the shitster tables, we get to keep the lot because no fukker in the US Treasury will ever know."

As the commencement of the global climate change summit for world leaders was not for another three days, Crump and I immersed ourselves in every cultural attraction Las Vegas had to offer. All in all, we lost a crapload of cash gambling at the casinos, frequented a multitude of dubious strip joints and notorious houses of ill repute, and ate more all-you-can-eat buffets than I care to remember. And so by the time the summit rolled around, as Bich liked to say, Crump and I were both worn slap out.

"Howdy, Mr. President, ya look like shit," called out Bich, who had just that moment entered the presidential penthouse suite with OnYurway and was giving us one of her oversized Arkansas grins. "Ya know when Cooter comes back from a night out drinkin' and whorin', Granny always gives him some of her chili and possum entrails pick me up, which usually does the trick. And as it happens, ya in luck because I've got a jar of the kickass fukkin stuff in my room, so hang tight, Mr. President, while I go and get it."

"Bich, you should know by now that I never eat or drink anything from goddamn Arkansas. Or any of the other shithole Southern States for that matter," snapped Crump, and then he opened a can of diet coke and sat down next to me on the sofa. "Just give me the details of this fukkin summit and when I'm supposed to be making the keynote address to the fukkers who turn up?"

"Ya on at two this afternoon, Mr. President. And because ya know next to nothin' about climate change, with OnYurway's help, I've spent the last three days writin' a shitdinger of a speech for ya," nodded Bich, with a grin. "There's also a gala dinner taking place tonight for all world leaders and the special guest speaker, so ya gonna be expected to attend. And then the summit continues for the rest of the week, which means there ain't goin' to be time for ya to do much else but sit on ya ass and listen to all them fukkers spout shit."

"Um, we'll see about that. I'm the leader of the free world, and this is fukkin Vegas. So I'll do as I goddamn well please," growled Crump, who at that moment was uploading our strip club selfies onto the official POTUS Facebook page. "And, Bich, which tree-hugging asshole have they chosen to be the guest speaker?"

"Mr. President, I'm afraid it's that annoyin' little shittosser from Greenland, Beretta Thornburger," answered Bich, while shrugging her shoulders and rolling her eyes.

"That's all I fukkin need. How did that bullcrapping assbite make it all the way here to Vegas? I thought the little fukker refused to fly because it's bad for the mothafukking environment, or so she claims. I've got a good mind to teach that shitstick a lesson by buying Greenland, exploiting its dicksneeze citizens, and mining the fuk out of the shithole," seethed Crump, as he typed a message on his phone to Skeeter Shiznit that I couldn't help but notice included the words, mad fukkers!

Beretta Thornburger, I found out, was a quick-witted 12-year-old gun-toting climate change activist who was hellbent on saving the planet. And it was true what Crump had said about her aversion to flying, which is why she chose to swim from her native Greenland to Canada before roller skating over 3,000 miles to the bright lights of Las Vegas.

Once we had finished binging ourselves on another Las Vegas buffet, the four of us rode in the Beast to the Las Vegas Convention Center for the global climate change summit. With the notable exceptions of China, Russia, and India, who along with the United States were the world's most prolific climate change contributors, pretty much every world leader, barring North Korea's, was in attendance.

Accompanied by a dozen Secret Service agents, Crump made his way to the podium, just as Bich, OnYurway, and I took our seats at the back of the stage. While the irony of hosting a climate change summit in Las Vegas was lost on most of the attendees who flew there in gas-guzzling private jets, it had not gone unnoticed by me. In point of fact, in large part due to its whopping electricity consumption, I discovered the carbon footprint of Las Vegas was greater than that of most countries, whose leaders, paradoxically, were in attendance.

Almost from the outset, Crump's carefully choreographed climate change speech went off track after he claimed the world was flat. Thinking the stunned silence resonating from the other world leaders meant everyone in the room agreed with him, he went on to say his administration was committed to the acceleration of global warming. Then, ignoring the jeers from nearly every attendee, and a resounding, "Fuk you, Crump," from Beretta Thornburger, Crump ended his keynote speech with a climate change pledge. And this, he proclaimed, was that under the leadership of Ronald S. Crump, the US of A would regain its #1 spot in carbon dioxide emissions by out polluting the fukkin Chinese.

"Crump, you fukhead, we're gathered here to combat global climate change. Not to make it worse," screeched Beretta Thornburger, who was waving her namesake Beretta M9 in the air, which she had purchased at a local convenience store only that morning. "As we speak, hurricanes are decimating the coast of Florida, and a whole load of tornadoes are tearing up Oklahoma, and it's all because of fukkin manmade climate change."

"Listen here, you little shitbagger, I speak for all Americans when I say, who gives a fuk! For nearly a century, the US of A has been the world leader in warming the planet, and I intend to keep it that way. If we left it to you goddamn tree huggers, we'd all be freezing our asses off by now. Just like you do in fukkin Greenland," taunted Crump, before turning towards me with a grin on his face and a thumb in the air. Then seeing Skeeter Shiznit had arrived with six hooded individuals, Crump gave the dirty trickster a nod of his head, and that's the moment when in a bat of an eye, all hell broke loose.

It was undoubtedly the mooing that caught the attention

of everyone at the summit. Before cries of mad fukkers rang out after Skeeter removed his companions' hoods and pushed them further into the room. As he hurriedly left by the front door, the Secret Service ushered Crump out the back, and Bich and I followed with OnYurway's magnums protecting our rear. Then looking over my shoulder, I saw quick on the draw Beretta Thornburger courageously gun down two mad fukkers before being bitten herself. At which point, I realized the global climate change summit for world leaders was now over.

"Trenton, I told you that we're not in Vegas for a lameass summit full of dickbeating fukwits. It's two more days of whoring and gambling for us before we head back to the Crump House," laughed Crump, as the heavily guarded presidential motorcade exited the Las Vegas Convention Center.

As always, Crump was true to his word. For the next couple of days, we overindulged in every vice that could be had in Las Vegas and then some. Then after our last night painting the proverbial town red, Crump and I wrecked the Playboy Hotel's presidential penthouse suite before heading back to McCarran International Airport in the Beast.

"All in all, Trenton, I'd say that was an assbender of a successful summit," yawned Crump, as he accepted a can of diet coke upon entering Air Force One and then sat down next to me.

"Mr. President, are ya sure that ya don't want any of this chili and possum entrails pick me up?" asked Bich, who was sitting across the table from us, drinking from a jar of the evil-smelling concoction. "It sure is tasty, and Granny always says that there's nothin' like it for sortin' out ya fukkin head."

"No, and if you ask me one more time, I'll order OnYurway to shoot you in your goddamn head," hissed Crump, who was

154

looking a little fragile after our week of Las Vegas revelry.

"Oh well, it's ya fukkin loss," shrugged Bich, and then she gulped down the entire contents of the jar before letting out a rather unpleasant belch. "Mr. President, ya know that those asscrackin' twisters are still whippin' up a whole shitheap of trouble in Oklahoma. And I understand that at this very moment, there's a real big fukker headin' for Tulsa. But don't worry. The captain has filed a flight plan that'll steer us well away from there and that pissass turbulence ya hate so much."

"Bich, I'll show those global warming doomsayers how Ronald S. Crump deals with a fukkin tornado," roared Crump, after slamming his can of diet coke down on the table. "Tell the captain to head to Tulsa at once, and when he catches sight of the fukker, I want him to give us a heads up and fly right over it."

To my surprise, not all of the overhead bins in Air Force One were used for luggage, as I had previously assumed. Instead, half of them contained an assortment of weapons of mass destruction acquired by former presidents. And this included one sizeable thermonuclear warhead gifted by the Kims during Crump's last vacation in North Korea. Crump, I very quickly found out, had come up with the idea of detonating the warhead inside the tornado with the aim, he so eloquently put it, of blowing the mothafukkin thing to Kingdom Come. And that is why Bich and OnYurway, along with my help, spent the next couple of hours carefully lowering a nuclear bomb to the floor of Air Force One before dragging it to one of the overwing exits.

Once we were nearing Tulsa, Air Force One descended to a lower altitude, and that's when the captain announced the tornado was dead ahead. With Crump barking his instructions while securely strapped to his seat, the cabin was depressurized so that I could disarm and pry open the exit door. The gist of Crump's plan being that on his command, the instant we were over our target, the pilots would roll Air Force One to one side so that Bich and OnYurway could push the bomb through the open hatch.

"Put your back into it, Bich," yelled Crump, and then he threw his empty can of diet coke at the Crump House press secretary. "We're directly over the goddamn tornado now, so push the mothafukker out."

"The darn thin' won't budge, Mr. President," screamed Bich, who, along with the strapping OnYurway, had been pushing with all her might while I held the door open. "It's just too big for the fukkin exit."

Hopping mad, Crump raised himself from his seat before stomping down the aisle to where we stood grappling with the nuclear bomb. Not willing to give in so easily, he ordered Bich through the open door so that she could stand on the wing and pull while he and OnYurway pushed from the inside. Realizing his press secretary was right for a change, Crump bellowed there would be a change of plan before instructing the captain to bring us around for another try. Then as soon as Bich was back inside Air Force One, and I had shut the exit door, the four of us hauled the bomb to the rear of the plane, where the presidential escape pod was to be found.

"Bich, the door release button is the green one on that control panel just behind you," spluttered Crump, as he was somewhat out of breath by the time we reached the escape pod. "Press the fukkin thing, and then we'll load this fukstick onboard."

"Righty-ho, Mr. President," nodded Bich, who, in the excitement of the moment, pressed the red launch button.

"Goddamnit, Bich, are you trying to give me a mindfuk?"

howled Crump, and then she pressed the green button after we saw the escape pod tumble to the ground.

"There's no need to worry, Mr. President, I'll ride the mothafukker right into that there twister. It'll be just like ridin' a fukkin greased hog at the Arkansas State Fair," replied Bich, who was sitting astride the bomb as we pushed it through the open hatch.

Then, after the three of us watched Bich ride the North Korean nuclear warhead into the center of the tornado, a mushroom cloud of debris and smoke rose over Tulsa, Oklahoma. And that's when Crump gave me a thumbs up and a smile before opening a congratulatory can of diet coke and telling the captain it was time we head home.

10

CRUMP on Pardons

"Only poor fukkers go to prison, the rich and famous buy pardons!"
— Ronald S. Crump, President of the United States

* * *

The day after returning from our eventful trip to Las Vegas, which included the short-lived global climate change summit for world leaders, laying waste to the City of Tulsa, and losing the Crump House press secretary in the process, Crump and I were once again sitting in the familiar surroundings of the Oval Office.

"Well, Trenton, it's back to the simple life for us," remarked Crump, as we sat at the Resolute desk eating our lunch of Crumpburgers and diet coke. "Apart from that assbagging memorial service we have to attend this afternoon, we've got nothing to do for the rest of the day. That means we can put our feet up, play a few games of snap and Twister, and listen to SHITE news to find out everything that's worth fukkin knowing."

"I have to say, the Crump House is not going to be the same without Bich Landers and her effervescent grin," I lamented, with a sigh and a shake of the head.

"Trenton, shit happens. Besides, I like to look on the bright side of all this. And that is it saves me having to shitcan the asshead," chuckled Crump, before he helped himself to a second Crumpburger. "What's more, finding another press secretary who is as dumb as Bich is going to be as easy as running against a fukkin Democrat for the presidency. And come to think of it, this is something you should jot down in that notepad of yours. If you're going to hire someone, then get the dumbest fukker you can find because they'll always make you look cleverer than you actually are."

At around 4 pm, Crump and I left the Oval Office to walk to the Rose Garden, which is where Bich's memorial service was to take place. As the Crump House press secretary had been vaporized in a thermonuclear explosion, I had come up with the idea of sending a keepsake of her back to Arkansas. So after lunch, I had emptied the contents of my cherished Earl Grey teabags into a used Crumpburger carton. Then after stamping it with the Great Seal of the United States and writing the words, BICH'S ASHES, Crump's new personal assistant sent it by overnight delivery to Granny Landers.

While the memorial service was undeniably a slapdash affair, it was enthusiastically attended by every member of the Crump House press team. Though I'm sure the pizza and cans of diet coke to be found on Bich's empty makeshift coffin had something to do with that. Then, along with Crump and I, there was Tribianka, Waywerd Pushover, and Asyphilis. And Oleander OnYurway was in attendance with her fully loaded magnums for a two-gun salute. Understandably, Birk was not present because he was still chained to the wall of the Crump House dungeon. But a coked-up Ronald Crump Jr. wearing a Christian Dior dress was there, as he had volunteered to preside over the ceremony.

"Dad, why is it the best of us so often go before their time?" uttered Waywerd, while wiping away a tear that was trickling down his cheek.

"I wish you would go, you goddamn asswipe. And it's Mr. President, to you," snapped Crump, before telling OnYurway to slap Waywerd across the face with the back of her hand. "If I hear you call me Dad one more time this afternoon, you'll end up in Bich's coffin with a bullet through that assbrained head of yours."

Cowering in fear of OnYurway's strong right hand, the Crump House chief of staff wisely retreated before joining the jovial crowd of mourners gathered around the coffin. Then after every slice of pizza had been eaten and the diet coke had run dry, Crump stepped forward to make a brief but sobering farewell speech in honor of his recently departed press secretary.

"I've known plenty of dumbass fukkers in my time, but I have to say that Bich Landers took the shitass biscuit," announced Crump, while pointing his finger at his eldest son. "Bich was truly a fukaholic of epic proportions, and as most of you well know, she wasn't my first choice for the job of Crump House press secretary. In truth, she was the 28th in a long line of chickenshit fukkers that I was forced to shitcan for one reason or another. And I would have done the same with Bich if it had not been for the fact that the Arkansas cumbubble believed the fukkin job was pro bono."

Following a rapturous round of applause from everyone

present, Crump made his way to the back of the small crowd where I was standing with my notepad and pen in hand. At that point in the service, once Jr. had snorted his way through several more lines of coke, Waywerd helped him climb on top of Bich's coffin to give the eulogy. As was his habit, rather than reminisce about the deceased Crump House press secretary, he spouted a whole load of incoherent narcissistic shit, which I chose not to jot down. It was about then I caught the whiff of something unmistakable, and that's when someone who had been standing behind us unnoticed tapped Crump on the shoulder.

"Howdy, Mr. President, and ya too, Trenton," called out an extremely disheveled and visibly glowing Bich Landers. Who, astonishingly, was standing before us with a grin on her face and clutching an open jar of redneck caviar. "What y'all bunch of fukkers doin'? Ya not havin' a hog roast without little ol' Bich are ya?"

In all the confusion, I wasn't sure which person screamed the loudest, Waywerd Pushover, who promptly fainted, or Ronald Crump Jr., as he fell from Bich's coffin. Not that it really mattered because the memorial service for the 28th Crump House press secretary was now quite clearly at an end. Evidently, Bich had survived her ride on the North Korean nuclear warhead and the subsequent thermonuclear explosion that destroyed much of Tulsa. And aside from some charring here and there, and a prominent radioactive glow, she let us know in no uncertain terms that her Arkansas ass was as right as fukkin rain.

It was several days before I saw Bich Landers again as Crump insisted his press secretary undergo a thorough radioactive decontamination by the Crump House medical team. In the meantime, the first doses of the MFD vaccine were ready to inoculate those Americans willing and able to pay. To avoid another mad fukker incident, like the one with Hank Krappa, Crump made sure everyone in the Crump House was first in line to get a shot of Crump. And though Crump, Tribianka, Asyphilis, and I received our shots of Crump for free, everyone else was forced to pay for them.

"Mr. President, those darn shitster doctors have given me the all-clear. So Bich's back and fukkin rarin' to go," hollered Bich, as she burst through the Oval Office door with Oleander OnYurway in tow. "Ya know that I hitched all the way back from Tulsa only to be prodded and poked. And then I had to bend over to get a bare-ass scrub down by a bunch of fukkers in white coats. All I can say is what a week, the last time I had this much fun was when I spat out a young'un sideways while drinkin' a jug of Granny's homemade hooch."

"Bich, I'm not going to say that your pitiful worthless ass has been missed around here because I can assure you it fukkin hasn't," replied Crump, who was sitting at the Resolute desk playing a game of snap with Tribianka. "Now, to what do I owe this visit? Or are you just popping by to waste my time and scratch my scrote as usual?"

"I sure did miss ya fukkin droll sense of humor, Mr. President," winked Bich, with a grin. "I'm here to remind ya that the goddamn SPATs are nearly upon us, so here's a copy of the trivia questions that'll be used in the first round quiz. For the past couple of months, Twatt Jabowsky has had his top people work around the clock on the answers. So be sure to memorize them because everyone at the Crump House is rootin' for ya to stick it to that Democratic fukker, Smilin' Mo Fudrucker."

"Bich, I didn't become a billionaire and the leader of the free world by fukkin studying. And besides, Twatt's going to be feeding me the answers through a dickass earpiece. So what the assfuk could possibly go wrong?" retorted Crump, before yelling snap and throwing his arms in the air. "Trenton, you know sometimes I think that I'd prefer having one of those old-fashioned shittossing debates with Fudrucker. That's because if you repeat the same thing over and over, even if it's a load of kissassing fukeroo, the goddamn electorate will lap it up and think it's true. Anyway, what I want to know is how's my fukjob of a pyramid coming along, and where are we with conversions to Crumpism?"

"Mr. President, ya gonna be over the cockass moon to know that accordin' to the overseers in the Secret Service, the Crump Monument is scheduled to be completed within the next two months. Although I have to say, work-related accidents and deaths on the pyramid are at an all-time high. Mind you, no one gives a shit about those fukkers because they're only undocumented immigrants," reported Bich, who was reading from her Crump House press diary. "And Archbishop Jacoff reports Crumpism is now the fastest-growin' religion in the country. He reckons that at this rate, by the end of the year, the Church of Crump will be one of ya biggest fukkin earners."

After Bich had finished speaking, I could see Crump was as pleased as fukkin punch that the completion of the Crump Monument was only around the corner. And the fact that he was making a shitload of cash out of the new national religion of Crumpism meant his spirits were as high as I had ever seen them. Then just as Crump began a new game of snap with Tribianka, I heard a timid sounding knock on the door, at which point, Waywerd Pushover strolled in carrying an enormous stack of manila folders.

"Hi, Dad, I've brought the presidential pardons for you to sign. We must have sold over 300 this month, which has got to be a record for any administration," exclaimed Waywerd, as he beamed at Crump while placing the manila folders on the Resolute desk. Then seeing Crump was giving him the fukeye, and OnYurway was fingering one of her magnums, the Crump House chief of staff swiftly exited the Oval Office without uttering another word.

I had read that the pardon racket, as it had become known over the years, was a popular perk of every US president since George Washington, and needless to say, Crump was no exception. It was a uniquely American governmental tradition in which a sitting president could pardon any and as many convicted felons as he or she wanted. And until the Crump presidency, it had primarily been used as a way to circumvent the country's internationally revered legal system. For no other reason, I discovered, than to get friends and family members off the hook and out of the federal slammer.

As one might expect, Crump had taken it to the next level by offering pardons to every high-net-worth jailbird in the federal penitentiary system. This was because Crump's presidential pardons didn't come cheap, so it was only the rich and famous who could afford them. Although the upshot of this was that with their get-out-of-jail cards only a Swiss bank transfer away, white-collar crime under the Crump administration soared. But as Crump so often pointed out to his critics in the fake press, federal courts stacked with Crump-appointed judges had no problem filling the empty cells with hardened criminals like fukkin shoplifters and jaywalkers.

"Trenton, you know that these presidential pardons can go for up to a million a pop. So as long as white-collar crime continues to rise, I'm going to be raking it in for a fukload of years to come," bragged Crump, while flexing his muscles before grasping OnYurway's hand to practice his arm wrestling. "Who'd have imagined the goddamn US legal system was going to make me more cash than Crumpburger brings in from the whole of fukkin Asia. And I'll tell you this, it's not just the pardon racket, I get to nominate the mothafukkin federal judges as well."

"Mr. President, that reminds me of somethin' Shifty Daniels requested when I last visited him in Sing Sing," interrupted Bich, who was sitting beside me on the sofa with her feet on the coffee table. "I'd plum forgot until now, but he wants to know when ya gonna grant him one of those presidential pardons? He's next in line to become the cell block bitch, so he wants to get his ass out of the fukkin slammer as soon as possible."

"Bich, while Shifty's sitting in Sing Sing, I get all the legal advice I need, but I don't have to pay the fukker a dime. So why the assdingo would I want to give him a presidential pardon? As far as I'm concerned, that goddamn fukweasel is going to be residing in the slammer for the next 20 years," barked Crump, after winning his arm wrestling match against OnYurway. "And as I was saying, I get to nominate all the judges in this shitster country, and for a dickrattling Supreme Court justice, that's an asscrazy tax-free $10 million for yours truly."

As I came from a country where the democratic institutions of government and the judiciary were totally separate, and never the twain shall meet, I was intrigued to hear that in the US of A, it was entirely the opposite. It had never occurred to me before that permitting politicians to interview and hire judges themselves for lifetime appointments allowed for a much more efficient legislative process than I had witnessed in England.

With judges in the politicians' pockets, legal oversight of the government by the judiciary was nigh on non-existent. And this meant that politicians could pretty much do as they fukkin well pleased, with none of the legal repercussions typically found in most other democratic countries to worry about.

For the rest of the afternoon, Crump continued practicing his arm wrestling with OnYurway before all five of us played an exhausting game of Twister. Then as we drank our cans of diet coke, Crump divvied up the manila folders sitting on the Resolute desk and handed a pile to everyone in the room except me. While Crump and the others signed his name on each of the presidential pardons, I sat next to Crump with my calculator to the ready. Under the watchful eye of my mentor, I then added up the dollar amount stated on every pardon so that Crumpburger's creative accountant could record the monies to be received as an off-the-books entry.

Over the next couple of weeks, Crump spent much of his time in training for the SPATs along with tweeting out all kinds of shit to his Crumper followers. Due to licensing agreements negotiated with every major pharmaceutical company, the MFD vaccine rollout was now moving along at what Crump ostentatiously liked to term, Warp Speed. Although more importantly to him, as people across the world began receiving their shot of Crump, a crapload of cash rolled into his numerous offshore bank accounts.

It wasn't all good news, as the General's reports from the MFD pandemic frontline painted a pretty dismal picture for the Crump campaign team. While the US Army had been successful in containing the onslaught of mad fukkers in Crumper country, regrettably, they had captured only a handful of them and had shot the rest. And though this wouldn't normally have concerned Crump in the least, Twatt Jabowsky pointed out, the dead were mostly ASS men, and as such, they were more than likely Crumpers.

When the big day had at last arrived, I was thrilled to learn that Crump had insisted I get a front-row seat to the Standardized Presidential Aptitude Tests. These were a uniquely American democratic affair to help the electorate determine which candidate had what it takes to run the US of A. And although the next president of the United States would be the candidate who received the most Electoral College votes in November, since 2024, no candidate had won the presidency without first winning the SPATs.

I was not the only one in the Crump House that was looking forward to the forth United States SPATs. The other was the Crump House press secretary, who, upon discovering they were to be held in Arkansas, hadn't stopped jabbering about the SPATs for weeks. Not only that, Buford P. Bucksnort had won the contract to host the event at Bucksnort Stadium, the home to Bich's beloved Little Rock Hyenas. Naturally, this had pleased Crump immensely because Crumpburger would be the exclusive caterer at the 50,000 attendee event.

With the exception of the grandiose presidential section of Air Force One, those seated in economy class, or shitass steerage as Crump preferred to call it, were packed in like sardines. Bich Landers and the rest of the Crump House press team were there, along with every fukker imaginable from the fake press and all three of the SHITE buddies. Then walled off from the others, and sitting in plush executive seats, were Crump and I, Asyphilis, Tribianka, Waywerd Pushover, Ronald Crump Jr., Oleander OnYurway, and an already liquored up Twatt Jabowsky.

The only seat not occupied on Air Force One had been reserved for Skeeter Shiznit. He wasn't currently sitting there because a week earlier, Mylo Peckerhead had been defeated in both the speed and agility and strength rounds of the vice presidential SPATs. It wasn't entirely the dirty trickster's fault though, because he had followed Crump's instructions to a T by having an associate break LSD's wrestling arm. Unfortunately, the dicksneeze had gone and broken the wrong fukkin arm. Needless to say, this had left Skeeter in the fukhouse, and his name was now at the top of Crump's list of fukkers that had aggrieved him.

"Twatt, this goddamn earpiece of yours better not break down," growled Crump, who had spent the last few minutes dreaming about blowing Skeeter Shiznit and the rest of the fukkers on his list to kingdom come with the anti-aircraft gun sitting in the Rose Garden.

"No need to worry about that, Mr. President," replied Twatt, as he took another swig from the jug of Kentucky moonshine he was holding in his hand. "That earpiece is nothing like the crap that comes out of California. No, siree, this one's designed and manufactured in fukkin North Korea."

After entering Arkansas airspace, we made our long descent into Little Rock before Air Force One landed at Clinton National Airport. Though I found it hard to believe, Crump informed me that it was named after an ex-president who had been caught with his pants down even more times than Mylo Peckerhead. Crump was to be greeted on the tarmac by the Republican Governor of Arkansas, a bunch of gun-toting ASS men, Buford P. Bucksnort, and every team member from the Little Rock Hyenas. However, things did not go quite as planned because Bich Landers, in an inexcusable breach of presidential protocol, was the first down the steps and promptly threw herself on the first Hyena she came across.

Once the formalities were over, with the heavily armed Arkansas National Guard positioned along our route, the largest presidential motorcade I had traveled in up to now departed for Bucksnort Stadium. As usual, Crump and I were seated in the Beast, along with Asyphilis and Tribianka. And there were Bradley Fighting Vehicles and M1 Abrams tanks to our front and rear. Not surprisingly, for an event of this magnitude, every agent the Secret Service could muster was on duty that day, and the skies were filled with so many armed drones that even the most ardent mad fukker stayed away.

By the time we arrived at Bucksnort Stadium, I could barely control my excitement, as I knew the candidate who emerged victorious would most likely be elected the next president of the world's oldest and best democracy. And I was all the more impassioned, knowing that every democratic country around the globe would be watching earnestly over the coming weeks as Americans unilaterally chose the self-proclaimed leader of the free world.

I had always been somewhat perplexed, though, by the American claim that their country was the oldest democracy in the world since it was not established until 1789. And being a scholar of history, I knew that while the Founding Fathers had declared all men equal, you had to count yourself amongst the 6% of white male landowners to vote. By comparison, the democratic ideals of my own unassuming country had been around since the signing of the Magna Carta in 1215. And when an overbearing and altogether conceited monarch challenged parliamentary rule way back in the 1600s, the people had famously lopped off the presumptuous fukker's head.

As Arkansas was overwhelmingly a diehard Crumper state, three-quarters of Bucksnort Stadium was filled with ASS cap wearing Crumpers. And, naturally, they had their concealed weapons and spare ammunition in readiness for the big event. Almost everyone was holding a Crumpburger in one hand and a paper cup containing a light beer or the soda of their choice in the other. And because the venue was owned by a top donor to the Crump campaign and Crumpburger franchisee, to Crump's delight, playing on a continuous loop and reverberating throughout the stadium was his signature soundtrack, Crump is Simply the Best.

Before the commencement of the main event, I was ushered to my VIP seat, and then a few minutes later, I was joined by Crump and his campaign manager. As we ate our Crumpburgers, Crump and I both drank diet coke while Twatt Jabowsky quietly supped his moonshine. We didn't have long to wait before the Little Rock Hyenas rewarded us with an exhibition game of catch to show off their ball-handling skills. And though it was plain to see why Little Rock's washed-out football team had not won a single game during the past 20 years, we all enjoyed ourselves immensely by throwing half-eaten Crumpburgers at the hopeless fukkers. Then to whip every Crumper in the stadium into a state of frenzy ahead of the first SPAT, a freestanding greased pole was wheeled in so that the first lady could perform her much-vaunted pole dancing routine.

Asyphilis's performance certainly did the trick as ASS caps were thrown into the air, and gunfire rang out throughout Bucksnort Stadium. It wasn't until the pole dance was over and an announcement made to refrain from shooting guns while in the stadium that the ruckus finally came to an end. Then as the lights started to flicker, Buford P. Bucksnort himself climbed onto the stage and proclaimed the forth United States SPATs would now begin.

"Well, Trenton, it looks like this is it. There's no need to wish me luck because Crump always wins. Just make sure that you take some shots of me trouncing that shittosser, and I'll upload them to the POTUS Facebook page when we're back in the Oval Office," said Crump, as he stood up and pointed to a group of four women standing in front of the small crowd of Democrat supporting never-Crumpers. "I was wondering when those bunch of clusterfuks would turn up, and Twatt, pay attention and have the answers to the fukkin questions ready because I'm on in a few minutes."

While Crump made his way to the stage, I could see that the women he was referring to were his long-time antagonists, the nefarious Posse. Each of them held pompoms in their hands and were decked out in Democrat blue uniforms, with the words, Go, Smilin' Joe, emblazoned on the front and back. From this distance, the silver-tongued LSD, who the Republicans and SHITE news so often vilified, was the most identifiable. And this was because the congresswoman was still wearing a plaster cast on the arm that Skeeter Shiznit's associate mistakenly broke.

Not wanting to be outdone by their nemesis, Ronald Crump Jr. stood facing the Posse on the other side of the stage and was dressed in a Republican red sequined ball gown and a top hat adorned with a red neon Crumpburger logo. He was joined by Dicker Polson, Ranting Prick Enderbee, and Vaj Ingersol of the SHITE buddies, along with Tribianka and a somewhat nervous-looking Waywerd Pushover. All of whom wore a similarly brash bodysuit, the same top hat, and just like Jr., they were holding a pair of pompoms with a letter on each that spelled out the words, FUK FUDRUCKER.

Sporting his signature smile, Smilin' Mo Fudrucker joined Crump on the stage, to a round of applause and chanting from the never-Crumpers, and a series of well-choreographed dance moves from the Posse. After they had finished, Crump's cheer-leading team strutted their stuff to the chants of Fuk Fudrucker from the 40,000 tumultuous Crumpers in the stadium. Then as the commotion died down and Crump and Smilin' Mo took their seats at opposite ends of a long table, Bich Landers called out, "Fudrucker, ya goddamn shitweasel, ya fukkin goin' down."

Upon noticing Crump's campaign manager had nodded off, I gave the drunkard a nudge because the SPATs were now officially underway. While Buford P. Bucksnort read out the 8th-grade trivia questions during the intelligence round, Twatt Jabowsky fed Crump the answers by speaking into a microphone concealed in the lapel of his Crumpburger jacket. And though his speech was more than a little slurred, I could see that Crump looked confident as he wrote down the answers to the questions, whereas Smilin' Mo Fudrucker appeared anxious and was shaking his head.

With my heart pounding, I was over the moon that I had been given this tremendous opportunity to observe firsthand, American democracy in action. As I listened in awe to the chanting that only grew louder as the SPATs advanced and the sound of automatic weapons fire, I began to understand why the US of A was the envy of the free world. Then as the first round came to a close, with his jug in hand, Twatt Jabowsky unceremoniously passed out on the stadium floor. While this meant I would have to watch the next two rounds on my lonesome, I knew that I would relish these as much as the first. For no other reason than Crump had told me, strength, along with speed and agility, and, of course, his unrivaled intellect, was what he fukkin excelled at in life.

Two hours later, Crump and I were sitting in the Beast for the second time that day, along with a still greased up Asyphilis and the cheerleading Tribianka. This time we sat in silence as the presidential motorcade left the carnage in Bucksnort Stadium and headed back to Clinton National Airport. Crump had his arms folded and was grimacing as I looked through the rear window to see a jug waving Twatt Jabowsky running some distance behind us. He was shouting something out loud, but his cries were drowned out by the myriad of riotous Crumpers who had taken it upon themselves to declare war on the Secret Service and Arkansas National Guard.

"That fukker's walking home, and when he gets back to the Crump House, it's the dungeon for him. And that other fukker, Skeeter Shiznit, is going to be joining him there," fumed Crump, as he half raised his arm and pointed his thumb over his right shoulder. "Trenton, if the speed and agility round had been Twister instead of fukkin snap, that assclown, Fudrucker, wouldn't have stood a chance."

I found it hard to believe that my beloved mentor had not only lost at snap, he had also tied the underdog Smilin' Mo Fudrucker at arm wrestling. And while the North Korean earpiece Crump was wearing during the intelligence round had not failed him for even a second, he had lost all the same. The reason for this was that all of Crump's answers to the 8th-grade trivia questions were unreservedly wrong. And this was because although the answers had been provided by Twatt Jabowsky's top people, it transpired that every one of them was a dumbfuk who had not made it past 7th-grade.

173

11

CRUMP on Space

"If dumbasses want to be blasted into oblivion, I say good riddance to the fukkers!"
— Ronald S. Crump, President of the United States

* * *

After Crump's crushing defeat in the SPATs at the hands of Smilin' Mo Fudrucker, over the next few days, Crump and I spent most of our time holed up in the Oval Office. While Crump made a daily appearance on the SHITE buddies to shitwag a host of left-wing deep state conspiracy theories, I helped him tweet out more of the same shit to his Crumper followers. And with damage control now in full swing, by the time the week came to a close, all but a handful of Crumpers around the country believed Crump had been the real winner of the fourth United States SPATs.

"Trenton, there are three words you should jot down in that notepad of yours, and make sure you underline each of them. NEVER ADMIT DEFEAT. If something doesn't go your way, just look for excuses and make up any shit that pops into your fukkin head. It works for me every time," confided Crump, while patting me on the shoulder.

On the Monday of the following week, as we ate our lunch of Crumpburgers and diet coke, Crump turned on the television to watch one of his favorite movies, the international blockbuster, Titanic. Although I had seen it many times before, in my ignorance, I had always thought the film was about a tragic accident at sea. However, luckily for me, Crump was able to put me straight regarding that by giving a running commentary as the two of us devoured a whole bucket of hot buttered popcorn.

"You know, Trenton, back then you had some clever fukkers living in England. They managed to build the biggest fukoff ship in the world and then shitbagged everyone into thinking the mothafukkin thing was unsinkable before insuring the crap out of it. Then for its maiden voyage, they hired a real fukhead to sink it, and he did that alright, by sailing into a goddamn iceberg. Imagine hitting an iceberg in the middle of the pissass Atlantic Ocean. It's like finding a needle in a fukkin haystack," laughed Crump, and then he switched the channel to SHITE news just as there was a knock on the Oval Office door.

"Howdy, Mr. President, it's good to see that ya back to ya old self again. Last week it looked like ya had a goddamn beaver stuck up ya ass," remarked Bich Landers, as she and Oleander OnYurway walked in and sat down on the sofa. "Just to let ya know, Twatt's back, and so I had him chained to the wall of the Crump House dungeon, just like ya ordered. Also, the fukker has been bitchassin me about his moonshine, so I gave him a jug on condition he runs ya re-election campaign from the fukkin dungeon."

"And where's Skeeter? I want that fukker locked up in the

dungeon as well," barked Crump, who was helping himself to another can of diet coke.

"Fuk knows, Mr. President. But when he turns up, the Secret Service has been instructed to throw him in the same cell as Twatt," replied Bich, with a grin and a nod of the head. "Anyhows, it's time for ya press briefin', so we better haul our asses down there right away before the fukkers turn the afternoon into a goddamn shitfest."

Ten minutes later, all four of us were once again in the crowded Fukkers Briefing Room. As Crump took his place at the podium, I sat next to Bich at the rear of the stage and watched as she noisily wolfed down a whole jar of redneck caviar. Meanwhile, OnYurway stood at the back of the room fingering her magnums with one eye on the occupants of the misbehaving fukkers section. Then after a call for fukkin quiet from Bich, Crump tossed the shit to the Crump House press corps by declaring himself the undisputed winner of the SPATs. Ostensibly, for no other reason than it would be impossible for him to lose against Smilin' Mo Fudrucker, which was greeted by bewildered looks from the fukkers in the fake press, and the usual solitary standing ovation from Vaj Ingersol of the SHITE buddies.

"Crump, you've got to be off your goddamn rocker to think that you won the SPATs," shouted Loudmouth Lonnie Laverty of SBC, from his seat in the misbehaving fukkers section. "Every one of us here was at Bucksnort Stadium and saw Smilin' Mo Fudrucker wipe the floor with you in the intelligence, and then the speed and agility round. And when it came to your much-touted arm wrestling prowess in the strength round, you had to make do with a fukkin draw. So how the fuk do you expect to win the presidential election in November when you can't even beat your opponent in the SPATs? I for one am going to be voting for Fudrucker, and I'll be telling SBC's listeners to do the same."

"Loudmouth, that's fukkin fake news, you ungrateful shit-wagger. Don't forget that I'm the one who brought you the MFD vaccine, and without your shot of Crump, you would have turned into one of those mad fukkers by now," yelled Crump, as he slammed his fists down on the podium.

"Yeah, but I hear on the grapevine, you're making a crapload out of it," responded Loudmouth Lonnie Laverty, while point-ing his finger at Crump. Although, those were the last words anyone heard him say that day because the Crump House press secretary ran to the back of the room and stabbed him in the chest with her Arkansas toothpick.

"That'll teach ya shitbreathin' fukkers in the fake press not to mess with the Crump House," scoffed Bich, as Stoner McCall carried his SBC colleague from the Fukkers Briefing Room to receive some much needed medical attention. "Now, the next and last question this afternoon better be unrelated to the shitster SPATs, or ya likely gonna get the same as fukkin Loudmouth."

"I have a question, Mr. President," called out Raz Alvarez of DNN, with her hand in the air. "The Crump House has claimed the devastation in Tulsa was caused by a solar flare due to the overuse of solar panels to generate electricity. However, according to all the experts, an explosion of this type and the resulting radioactive fallout could only have originated from the detonation of a thermonuclear warhead. So, Mr. President, I think every American would like to hear what you have to say about that?"

"Listen, Raz, I've got no time for any of those shitbrained

experts. I happen to know more than the lot of them put together. And I can assure you, this so-called green energy is what caused that fukbanger of an explosion in Tulsa," retorted Crump, who then turned around to give me a wink. "This just goes to show what I and the good people in the coal, oil, and gas lobby have been saying for years. America needs to be 100% reliant on shitkicking fossil fuels. And with the notable exception of nuclear power, we should do away with the fukkin rest."

The following afternoon, Crump, Tribianka, and I sat at the Resolute desk with nothing to do but watch SHITE news and dial random numbers on the presidential phone. Moreover, if someone answered, we shouted, fukker, as loud as we could, then hung up and laughed our asses off before dialing another number. And we probably would have continued this for the remainder of the day, if Bich Landers and Oleander OnYurway had not burst through the Oval Office door with some important news.

"We're fukked, Mr. President," blurted Bich, with a half-eaten Crumpburger in one hand and a sheet of paper in the other. "Twatt's run the numbers, and he reckons there ain't enough Crumpers for ya to win the election. It looks like the General shot too many of the fukkers, and now there's not enough fukkin time to replace 'em."

"Daddy, you should force the never-Crumpers and undecideds to vote for you," squealed Tribianka, as she stamped her feet on the floor in an impromptu fit of hysterics.

"That's my little girl, always thinking of her Daddy," winked Crump, while slapping Tribianka on the ass. "Of course, we need to make the jackasses believe this goddamn country still has a semblance of democracy. So what does my fukwizard of a campaign manager propose we do?"

"Oh, Twatt doesn't have a fukkin clue. And there's no point in ya askin' me, I'm plum out of ideas," answered Bich, as she took another bite out of her Crumpburger.

"Well, that's nothing new. I surround myself with dumb-asses, and this is what I get," fretted Crump, who was slowly shaking his head. "Trenton, how about you. Can you think of anything?"

As Crump leaned back on his chair and the room went silent, I racked my brain for all it was worth, and at first, I came up with nothing. Then, out of the blue, something crashed into the Oval Office door, and so I walked to the other side of the room to open it. To my surprise, it was Crump's youngest son, Birk, who had been released from the Crump House dungeon to make room for Twatt Jabowsky. After I looked him over to ensure he was uninjured, Birk got back on his tricycle and rode off down the corridor shrieking, "I'm going to the Moon." And that's when the idea came to me.

"I know what we should do," I said, as I stood before Crump with a smile on my face. "We need a JFK moment to get every voter in the country behind you before the presidential election in November, no matter whether they be Crumper, undecided or never-Crumper. Remember the speech he made to Congress in 1961 about landing a man on the Moon and returning him safely to Earth. Why don't we do something like that, but instead of the Moon, because that's already been done, it should be Mars. That'll surely distract every fukker in the country and whip up enough nationalistic zeal to put Smilin' Mo Fudrucker out of the running for president."

"Trenton, that's a fukkin jackpot of an idea. As usual, just when I'm knee-deep in fukstruck assclowns, I can always rely on my presidential intern, Trenton Begby," smiled Crump, as he shook my hand. "You know, this is going to be a job for the General. He's still chasing after mad fukkers in one of those shitjob Southern States, but I'll give Merv a call and have him come to the Crump House right away."

A couple of days later, Crump and I had just finished our lunch of Crumpburgers and diet coke and were about to call Tribianka for a game of Twister, when there was a knock on the Oval Office door. As expected, it was the chairman of the Joint Chiefs of Staff, General Merv Shizerstrom. Instead of his regular dress uniform, he was wearing camouflage military fatigues with a liberal splattering of blood. And in place of a standard US Army sidearm, as always, he was carrying his toolbox containing a plunger and a bottle of industrial-strength bleach.

"I have to tell you, Mr. President, there were no shitters for me to clean on the MFD pandemic frontline. When you're in the thick of it, you just dig a hole and do it where you please. So I thought I'd give the Crump House shitters the Shizerstrom once-over while I'm here," announced the General, who had placed his toolbox on the Resolute desk and was now saluting Crump with his right hand while holding a plunger in the left.

"Merv, they'll be plenty of time for that later," acknowledged Crump, with a cursory wave of his hand. "I hear that your boys bagged themselves a shitload of mad fukkers over the past few weeks."

"That's right, Mr. President. It got to the point where we couldn't tell mad fukkers from regular fukkers. So in the end, I just ordered them to shoot anyone wearing an ASS cap," disclosed the General, as he returned the plunger to his toolbox. "And Dic Hade tells me that gun and ammunition sales have increased by over 50% since the pandemic began. Obviously,

ASS is losing members, but he knows that in the good ol' US of A, ASS can always recruit more gun-toting nutjobs to become ASS men."

"Excellent job, Merv. You've done a great service to your country. Now, how about this mission to Mars?" asked Crump, while helping himself to another can of diet coke.

"Well, Mr. President, I've spoken to NASA, and it's definitely doable," nodded the General, who was still standing to attention as he spoke to Crump. "Although the reason NASA hasn't attempted a mission like this before is that the rocket can only carry enough fuel to get there. And that means whoever volunteers for this mission ain't going to be coming back to Earth anytime soon."

"Mr. President, that sounds like a suicide mission to me. Can I go?" interrupted Bich, as she jumped up and down on the sofa with her hand in the air.

"Good idea, Bich," replied Crump, with obvious enthusiasm. "Merv, how many fukkers can this goddamn rocket take?"

"The command module can only hold two and no more, Mr. President," responded the General, who by now had an even sterner look on his face than usual. "And because this is likely to be a one-way trip, I believe we need a couple of all American heroes from the Space Cowboys for this mission. Trust me; a futile death all alone in the vastness of space is exactly what every Space Cowboy joined up for."

"Nonsense, Merv. Trust is for assholes. But tell me, do you need any technical ability to fly this mothafukker?" inquired Crump, after rejecting the General's recommendation out of hand.

"None at all, Mr. President. NASA told me that if you're dumb enough to want to be strapped to a bomb containing a million gallons of highly explosive rocket fuel and be blasted out into space, then it's unlikely you'll have the brains to pilot the fukkin thing," explained the General, in earnest. "From what I can comprehend, they point you in the right direction, and then you just sit back while mission control ignites the fuel in the engines and the onboard computer pretty much does the rest."

"In that case, what we need for this mission is a couple of expendable dumbfuks. And as it happens, I have the perfect fukkers in mind," smiled Crump, while nodding his head. "Merv, my only scrote itch I get from all this is that we can't squeeze Bich into the fukkin command module as well."

Once Crump had given the green light for the first-ever manned mission to Mars, he instructed NASA to prepare the rocket for a 7-day launch, which, conveniently, would allow the General plenty of time to clean the Crump House shitters before liftoff. As Bich wanted to make her Granny proud by being the first Landers to be launched into space, Crump offered her a seat on the next mission to Valhalla that came along. Then knowing he should make an announcement as soon as possible, Crump adjourned our game of Twister to address the nation.

With every major national news network present and their cameras rolling, a beaming Crump took his place at the podium in the Fukkers Briefing Room. Thankfully, the disruptive Loudmouth Lonnie Laverty was still recovering from his recent injury in a nearby hospital. So the only fukker in the misbehaving fukkers section that Oleander OnYurway had to keep her eye on was Jem Tossa of NBS. After receiving a nod from Crump, OnYurway fired her magnums into the air to silence the chattering reporters. Then, after Bich and I gave an improvised drum roll, Crump raised his arms and began his momentous

JFK-style speech.

"I decree this goddamn nation I rule will achieve the goal, before the week is out, of sending two fukkers into space to travel to that shitdinger of a planet called Mars. But let me tell you this, in a very real sense it will not be two fukkers going to Mars, it will be an entire nation of fukkers. For all of you lameasses out there must pay a fukload more tax to send them there," proclaimed Crump, and then Bich, OnYurway, and I, along with all three of the SHITE buddies, got to our feet and clapped. While the fukkers in the fake press remained seated and simply gazed at Crump in disbelieving silence. "Now, do any of you shitbaggers have any questions before I call it a day?"

"But why?" called out Mallory Hightower of CPR, without bothering to raise her hand. "How will sending two brave Americans to Mars benefit humanity?"

"Mallory, you shitwitted decrepit old fuktart. Who gives a flying assfuk about humanity?" retorted Crump, who then turned to me with raised eyebrows before shaking his head. "I'm sending the fukkers there to claim Mars for Crump."

"And who are the two courageous souls that have volunteered for this perilous mission?" asked Raz Alvarez of DNN, using a glib tone of voice that was clearly intended to be sarcastic.

"Raz, I'm glad you brought that fukkin question up," confirmed Crump, as he placed a hand across his face to conceal a smirk. "I can now announce to the world that in seven short days, I'll be bidding a fond farewell to my own dear sons, Birk and Ronald Crump Jr. It's a sacrifice on my part, I know, but I cannot ask others to do what I'm unwilling to do myself. So with a heavy heart, I have decided to launch the two fukkers into outer space where they can journey all the way to that far-off fukhole, Mars."

"Mr. President, do you mean to tell us your habitually coked-up elder son, and his younger brother, the woefully unqualified head of NASA, are going to pilot a technically advanced billion-dollar rocket to Mars?" implored Stoner McCall of SBC, who had his hands in the air as he spoke. "As far as I'm aware, neither of them is a qualified astronaut. And Ronald Crump Jr. has written off 27 cars over the past two years, while Birk is so inept, after 54 recorded attempts, he hasn't been able to pass a fukkin driving test yet."

"Stoner, if you were a real reporter like the three SHITE buddies sitting beside you and not just asscandy, you'd know that any dickwad can ride a fukkin rocket to anywhere. The hard part is always bringing the fukkers back. And I'll tell you this for nothing, I've got no intention of charging NASA with that," disclosed Crump, with a grin.

After Crump had put the fukkers in the fake press in their place, Dicker Polson gave one of his all too common asslicking speeches praising Crump's leadership. He was followed by his fellow SHITE buddie, Prick Enderbee, who ranted for a good five minutes about Smilin' Mo Fudrucker and the left-wing deep state. Then just as the briefing was coming to a close, Vaj Ingersol announced she was converting to Crumpism, as she believed the Church of Crump was God's true home on Earth.

"Hi, Dad, I heard from Tribianka, Birk and I will be going to Mars next week," remarked Ronald Crump Jr., as he walked into the Oval Office later that afternoon wearing a Dolce and Gabbana sleeveless dress and smoking a pipe. "I guess this means I'll be getting a raise?"

"Then you guess wrong, you fukwitted assbite," snapped Crump, who was sitting at the Resolute desk watching SHITE news, and, naturally, I was by his side. "I don't pay you a goddamn dime now, and that's not going to change just because you and your scatterbrained brother are leaving for a trip to Mars. Jr., look at it as an all-inclusive vacation paid for by the fukkin US taxpayer."

"In that case, Dad, you can rely on me. I've already started packing my best dresses for the trip. And I'll take plenty of photos when we're there so that you and Tribianka can see what the red planet looks like on our return," nodded Jr., just as a grinning Crump turned to me and winked.

It couldn't have been more than a couple of minutes after Ronald Crump Jr. had left when the door opened once again, and Tribianka strolled in. She wasn't alone as in her shadow I could see the familiar sight of the tricycle riding Birk. However, it was to be no more than a fleeting visit from the head of NASA, as he rode three times around the room and then shrieked, "I'm going to the Moon," before leaving the Oval Office to return to his playroom in the East Wing.

Over the coming days, while NASA prepped the rocket for launch at Cape Canaveral's Kennedy Space Center, Crump spent his time tweeting shit from the Resolute desk and making several appearances on the SHITE buddies. Surprisingly, in between briefings from the General and our innumerable games of Twister, Crump and I managed to find the time to name the rocket. As Crump was the 47th President of the United States, I came up with the name Crump 47, which Crump approved of as long as it accompanied a prominent red Crumpburger logo. And this, of course, had to be painted on both sides of the rocket.

As I had hoped, within hours of his address to the nation in which he announced his intention to send a mission to Mars, Crump's popularity across the remaining 48 states of the Union began what was to be a weeklong meteoric rise. On the eve of the launch, with a renewed nationalistic fervor sweeping across the country, Twatt Jabowsky and the Republican pollsters reported most undecideds were again leaning towards Crump. Now that the winner of the SPATs, Smilin' Mo Fudrucker, was losing ground fast, it appeared to all of us in the Crump House that as long as there was no assdingo of a calamitous fukup, Crump would assuredly win the presidential election to start his third term in office.

It wasn't long before the historic day was at last upon us. And as Crump considered Florida no more than a shitfilthy swamp filled with rednecks, old fukkers, and countless ASS men, he chose to watch the launch from the comfort and relative safety of the Oval Office. Needless to say, he wasn't alone as sitting on the sofa with party poppers in hand was Tribianka, Asyphilis, Waywerd Pushover, and as you would expect, yours truly, Trenton Begby.

If you supposed that we were watching the launch on SHITE news, then you would be right. In fact, the SHITE buddies were hosting their show live from the Kennedy Space Center and had just finished commenting on the christening of Crump 47 by Archbishop Dwight Jacoff. The Archbishop then gave a sales pitch to SHITE viewers on the benefits of Crumpism, including the offer of a free Crumpburger, when Vaj Ingersol cut in to announce Birk and Ronald Crump Jr. were about to board the rocket.

With a microphone in one hand and a Vote Crump placard in the other, the SHITE buddie could be seen running across the tarmac to Crump 47 to catch the parting words from the mouths of the heroic astronauts. Both of them were sporting a pair of official NASA mirrored sunglasses and held Crumpburger logoed space helmets. And wearing a wedding dress, Ronald

Crump Jr. was pushing a luggage cart with six oversize suitcases. Birk, on the other hand, wore what appeared to be a bunny suit and was riding his tricycle with his favorite teddy bear sitting astride the handlebars. As his elder brother looked too coked-up to form a coherent sentence, it was left up to the head of NASA to give the customary farewell speech to the world.

"I'm going to the Moon," shrieked Birk, with an idiotic grin on his face and two thumbs-up.

"No, you're not, you goddamn moron. You're going to fukkin Mars," yelled Crump, then he proceeded to throw a handful of popcorn at the television screen.

"Dad, it's an easy mistake to make," uttered Waywerd Pushover, who was sitting beside Tribianka. "You've got to admit, they're both round and begin with the letter M."

"Waywerd, you dickwaving assmonkey, I told you not to call me that," glowered Crump, while pointing a finger at his son-in-law. "And that reminds me, you'll be joining Bich on NASA's next pissass mission."

"But, I'm afraid of heights," trembled Waywerd, whose face was now as white as a freshly laundered Crump House bed sheet.

"Then keep your fukkin eyes shut," hissed Crump, as he threw an empty can of diet coke at the Crump House chief of staff before opening a new one for himself.

The next hour was taken up with loading Ronald Crump Jr.'s luggage and Birk's tricycle into the cargo bay of Crump 47, during which NASA completed a series of pre-flight checks. As this was about as boring as watching Bich Landers clean her fingernails with an Arkansas toothpick, SHITE news switched to a Crumpburger commercial break every three minutes. Then just as Crump, Tribianka, Asyphilis, and I became entangled in a game of Twister, Waywerd squawked from the sofa, the countdown had begun.

With each of us holding a party popper, we crowded around the huge wall-mounted television and listened as NASA commenced their countdown. I could see Birk waving from one of the rocket's windows, and then SHITE news switched to the onboard webcam. Inside the command module, Ronald Crump Jr. was using a cocktail shaker to fix himself a stiff vodka martini before departure. Then as the world looked on, he placed a couple of lines of coke on the rocket's idiot-proof control panel before tooting the shit up his nose.

It was only moments later that we heard the glorious words, "Liftoff! We have a liftoff," and Crump 47 with its two astronauts onboard was gracefully launched into the heavens. Then as everyone pulled their party poppers in unison, confetti flew in every direction. After which, all of us in the room gave Crump a round of congratulatory praise for another job well done.

"Well, that's the last we'll be seeing of those worthless fukkers," exclaimed Crump, as he turned off the television and smiled while rubbing his hands together with glee. "Now, let's play another game of Twister. And Waywerd, you asswipe, you can slope off back to whatever fukkin job you do around here."

Once Waywerd Pushover had left the room, the four of us played two more games of Twister. Then about an hour after Crump 47 had lifted off to begin its long voyage to Mars, Crump ordered a large bucket containing ice and a dozen cans of diet coke. As Crump, Tribianka, and I chatted, Asyphilis looked on in silence while sucking on an ice cube. It was at that moment, a pie-eyed Bich Landers startled us all by bursting through the door of the Oval Office with Oleander OnYurway not far behind.

"The shit's well and truly hit the fan this time, Mr. President," blurted Bich, who, with a jug of her Granny's homemade hooch, had been in the Crump House press office toasting the successful launch of Crump 47. "I've just heard from NASA that there's been a dicker of a mishap with that goddamn rocket of theirs."

"Bich, what the fuk do you want me to do about it now? You know that I never work past five. So tell the fukkers at NASA, I'll make another shitass address to the nation tomorrow afternoon," yawned Crump, as he shook his head in dismay. "And make sure my speech includes the usual bullcrap about their lives were not lost in vain. Oh yes, and their sacrifice was for the greater good or some shit like that. That'll surely get me the fukkin sympathy vote if nothing else."

"I sure can, Mr. President, but Ronald Crump Jr. and Birk ain't dead. Accordin' to the top dickrattlers at NASA, Jr. placed Birk's used diaper on the control panel, and its contents leaked into the rocket's shitster guidance system. And that sent the big fukker way off course and into an indefinite low orbit around Earth," disclosed Bich, with a half-hearted grin. "NASA said a rescue mission could take fukkin years to get underway. But luckily for the boys, Crump 47 holds enough food, water, booze, and shit for Jr. for them to live on for 25 years if need be."

"What! I'm not spending the next quarter of a century looking up at the stars, only to see those two grinning fukheads staring back at me," bellowed Crump, who was waving his arms in the air. "Trenton, get the General on the line, and I'll have him shoot the fukkers down."

As it turned out, hitting a rocket traveling at 25,000 miles an hour some 1,000 miles above the surface of the Earth was no mean feat. It took NASA almost a week to calculate the trajectory and for the US Air Force to program the coordinates into the longest-range thermonuclear ballistic missile that could be had. And because the missile was of North Korean design and manufacture, the launch site was located just outside Pyongyang. In the grounds of the inaptly named People's Palace, which happened to be the home of Crump's long-time friends and business associates, the Kims.

Being that Crump was never one to miss out on an opportunity to make a fast buck, he arranged for the missile to hit Crump 47 while orbiting the US Eastern Seaboard at precisely 10 pm EST. Then promoting it as the light show of the century, he arranged for an invitation-only party for the rich and famous to be held at Kiss-my-Ass. With a cover charge of $10,000 a head, attendees would receive an all-you-can-eat Crumpburger buffet and unlimited booze. And entertainment included a pole dancing Asyphilis followed by the wannabe Crumper and Canadian teen singing sensation, Rusty Beaver.

"Merv, I don't want any fukups today. This fukker better come down as planned, or it's back to the Crumpburger shitters for you," declared Crump, as we sat drinking diet coke aboard Air Force One on the day of the party.

"There's no need to worry, Mr. President. Everything's under control. Trust me, when that missile hits the rocket, it's going to look just like the Fourth of July," saluted the General, who had raised himself from his seat and was standing to attention. "The North Koreans assure me that anything not vaporized on impact will harmlessly burn up in the atmosphere to give us the high altitude firework display you requested."

"That's just what I want to hear, Merv, I knew that I can always count on you. Not like the other dickless asslickers that work for me," nodded Crump, and then he called to his press secretary. "Bich, did you shitwag those fukkers in the fake press as I asked you to?"

"Yes, siree, Mr. President, I sure did," grinned Bich, who was sitting beside OnYurway and snacking on a jar of redneck caviar. "I told 'em we're launchin' a rescue mission, and the fukkin dickweasels believed me."

To say that I was looking forward to the party at Crump's private members-only club and luxury island resort in the Caribbean would have been a gargantuan understatement. And as the evening unfolded, the memorable events of that day did not disappoint me in the least. Due to safety concerns about firing guns into the air and hitting someone who mattered, ASS men and weapons were prohibited at Kiss-my-Ass. This allowed Crump and I to do without our requisite bulletproof vests and mingle freely with the rich and famous, and, not unexpectedly, just about every high net worth white-collar criminal known to man.

"Well, Trenton, this is going to be something you don't see every day," chuckled Crump, as we drank from our cans of diet coke just before the anointed time of 10 pm. And along with everyone else attending the party, after Bich had announced the successful launch of the missile by the North Koreans, we were looking up at the stars beside the resort's main swimming pool.

Although unusually for Crump, except for shaking his head and uttering the word, FUKKERS, those were the last words he said to me that evening. That was because, after a faraway flash of light and a somewhat muted firework display, disgruntled mutterings could be heard before several of Crump's guests pointed upwards towards the night sky. As I gazed into the darkness to see what all the fuss was about, I saw three parachutes tethered to a large metallic object in the shape of a truncated cone. Recognizing it as Crump 47's command module, I watched as it crashed through the roof of Kiss-my-Ass and nigh on demolished the entire building. Then out of the ruins, a bunny-suited astronaut came into view and casually inquired, "Is this the Moon?"

12

CRUMP'ed

"Playing by the rules is for pussyfooting losers. That's why bil-lionaires never do!"
— Ronald S. Crump, President of the United States

* * *

"Mr. President, that sure was an assdingo of a calamitous fukup we had last week," exclaimed Bich Landers, who was sporting her customary grin as she entered the Oval Office with Oleander OnYurway. "But at least ya got ya boys back, and even those fukkers in the fake press had to admit the rescue mission was a dickwavin' fukkin success."

"Success! They think it was a goddamn success," yelled Crump, before throwing an unopened can of diet coke at Bich. Although, he missed the Crump House press secretary and struck OnYurway's amply cushioned chest instead. "Bich, I didn't want those two shitstains back in the first place, and now the fukkers have gone and destroyed Kiss-my-Ass. The only consolation was that almost everyone thought it was part of the fukkin show, so thankfully, I didn't have to refund a dickbeating dime."

"Oh well, as Granny likes to say, shit always happens when there's a Landers around," grinned Bich, as she sat down on the sofa and took a bite out of the possum fritter she was holding in her hand.

Since our return to the Crump House after the disastrous evening of the previous week, Crump and I had pretty much kept ourselves to ourselves by hanging out in the Oval Office. Except for watching SHITE news and playing Twister with Tribianka, Crump's time had been spent belittling his asswitted sons and tweeting out all kinds of unabridged foul-mouthed shit about Smilin' Mo Fudrucker. Then after several days of fuming about his once beautiful and now ruined Kiss-my-Ass, he ultimately cheered himself up by declaring a state of emergency.

Despite the fact that Kiss-my-Ass was located outside of US territorial waters and in actuality came under the jurisdiction of Mexico, it didn't stop Crump from proclaiming the island a national disaster. This meant he could rebuild his private members-only club and luxury island resort in the Caribbean using FEMA's Disaster Relief Fund. And not only that, because he wasn't paying for it himself, Crump let me know in no uncertain terms, the new Kiss-my-Ass would be a whole lot bigger and a fukload more palatial than before.

Meanwhile, after undergoing an exhaustive medical examination by a team of doctors from NASA, Birk and Ronald Crump Jr. had been pronounced physically A-OK and were returned to the Crump House. Though it was no surprise to Crump and me the two dumbfuks failed their basic mental capacity assessment, and so NASA had been forced to label them extraordinarily fukkin incompetent. Not that he needed one, but this gave Crump the perfect excuse to lock them up in the Crump House dungeon. And this is when Tribianka, without the slightest hesitation, obligingly volunteered to be their jailer.

As the small Crump House dungeon could comfortably accommodate only two fukkers at a time, Crump grudgingly agreed that Twatt Jabowsky should be released on probation. Then with the timely return of Skeeter Shiznit to the West Wing, he rather generously gave the two of them one more chance to redeem themselves. So with November rapidly approaching, Crump's campaign manager and dirty trickster were assigned to what could only be described as electioneering skulduggery.

Understandably, General Merv Shizerstrom had been demoted and was now working at Crumpburger on shitter duty. Where Crump assured him, he could work his way up the corporate ladder to get his old job back as Vice President of Sanitation in as little as 25 years. While this was definitely no hardship for the General, who had always been more at home with a plunger and a bottle of industrial-strength bleach than a gun, it was not so for his replacement. That was because Crump, in a moment of malevolent inspiration, made Waywerd Pushover the acting chairman of the Joint Chiefs of Staff. And then, with a great deal of joy and satisfaction on his part, ordered the fukker to get his ass down to the MFD pandemic frontline without delay.

Considering Birk and Ronald Crump Jr. had laid waste to Kiss-my-Ass with hundreds of paying onlookers in attendance, it had been a surprise to us all to learn that by the time the evening drew to a close, there was only one person not accounted for. So with bated breath, many a young fan across the globe had to wait days in earnest as the Secret Service searched for their beloved Rusty Beaver. Who, as it turned out, at the stroke of ten on that ill-fated day had been up to no good in one of the Kiss-my-Ass shitters.

"Well, they just found that lameass kid, or at least what's left of him," scoffed Crump, after he had finished reading a text message from the Secret Service. "Though I really don't know why they bothered. Let's face it, the fukker was Canadian, so who gives a shit."

"Goddamnit, that's another one I'll have to cross off my marriage bucket list," lamented Bich, with a sigh and a shake of the head. "Ya know his Beaverettes are gonna be fukkin heartbroken, all 10 million of 'em. And, Mr. President, I had Rusty lined up to sing at the openin' of the Crump Monument next month."

"Bich, it's your job to find a replacement, so get your ass in gear and don't fuk it up," barked Crump, as he helped himself to another can of diet coke. "And why you're about it, tell FEMA I want additional funds to construct a small but expensive memorial in remembrance of that fukker."

"Mr. President, that sure is thoughtful of ya," replied Bich, who was nodding her head while writing everything down in her Crump House diary.

"I'll have it built at the other end of the island, as far away from Kiss-my-Ass as possible. Then I'll charge those goddamn Beaverettes $100 a head to visit the fukkin memorial. It'll bring in millions, and every tax-free shittin penny will be for me," chuckled Crump, as he leaned back on his chair and smiled.

As the all-important month of November was rapidly approaching and the presidential election nearly upon us, with the notable exception of Crump, everyone in the Crump House quite literally was on tenterhooks. Not that they gave a shit about Crump, but losing to Smilin' Mo Fudrucker would undoubtedly mean every last one of them would lose their cushy and invariably lucrative jobs to people that were actually qualified to do them.

Even though every last Crumper in the country would assuredly vote Crump, no matter what cockamamie thing he did or said, others in the Republican Party had their misgivings. His loss at the SPATs had done nothing to bolster their confidence in him, and the Republican Party leadership knew all too well that every dead mad fukker meant one fewer registered Republican. And with the failure of the mission to Mars, alarmingly, the polls indicated undecideds were now favoring Smilin' Mo Fudrucker.

With that all said and done, everything was certainly not lost as Crump's campaign manager and dirty trickster were hard at work scouring cemeteries in every far-flung Crumper state to register the dead as Republican voters. Then with the Crump House 3D printers working around the clock, fake IDs were created so that Skeeter Shiznit's unprincipled associates could assume their identities and vote for Crump in November.

At the same time, changes were afoot at the highest echelon of the Crump House because Crump had finally had enough of his dickstick vice president. As LSD had bettered him in the vice presidential SPATs, and now that most evangelicals were converts to Crumpism, Crump had happily shitcanned the fukker. His replacement was Crump's top pick and always preferred choice, his most senior advisor, Tribianka. Mylo Peckerhead, though, was not entirely out of the Crump sphere of influence as he accepted a position as the Bishop of the Church of Crump in Jackson, Mississippi. And because of this, he was able to realize his longtime ambition of becoming a Crumpburger franchisee.

Crump and I were not idle in the least during this frenetic time as we spent our days watching SHITE news in the Oval Office and fabricating conspiracy theories, which Crump then tweeted out on a daily basis. As work and no play is no goddamn fun at all, or so the old saying goes, I introduced Crump and Tribianka to a game I had played as a child growing up in England. To my delight, they took to knock and nash like fish to water, and Crump even added his own Crumpian twist to the popular English childhood game. So as we ran down the corridors of the West Wing banging on office doors, we yelled fukkers at their occupants before running back to the Oval Office. Afterward, the three of us laughed our asses off as we drank cans of diet coke, and then as you might well guess, we did the same all over again.

Although we were uncommonly busy in the Crump House during the final days of Crump's re-election campaign, we had several televised rallies in Crumper country to attend as well. And as Florida was now the only swing state in the Union, being that Crump had returned Texas to Mexico, Twatt Jabowsky urged Crump to do a whole lot of shitwagging down there too. So once again, accompanied by Bich Landers and Oleander OnYurway, we boarded Air Force One wearing our Crumpburger caps for one last jaunt before Election Day.

Predictably, as almost everyone in attendance was an ASS cap wearing Crumper, the rallies were exceptionally well received, with only a smattering of hecklers here and there. Needless to say, each of them was swiftly dealt with by an ASS man with a gun, and as the only food sold at each venue was from Crumpburger, Crump, naturally, made a crapload of cash to boot. It wasn't all politics, though, because Crump always wrapped up his speeches with a few well-chosen words advocating Crumpism. And as the head of the Church of Crump, to his amusement, he was able to charge his campaign fund a tax-free quarter of a million for each appearance.

After our final stop in Florida, we returned to the Crump House, and, as usual, Crump and I were to be found in the Oval Office, shooting the breeze with Tribianka. It was the day before the opening of the newly completed Crump Monument, and Crump had just finished telling us that he considered it to be the crowning glory of the Crump business empire. I was abuzz with excitement as the day was to include an aerial display by the US Air Force and a kickass military parade at the National Mall. Then just as Crump switched on the television to receive his daily briefing from SHITE news, there was a knock on the door, and in strode Bich Landers and Oleander OnYurway.

"Mr. President, I got 'em," called out Bich, who was grinning from ear to ear as she waved a piece of paper at Crump.

"Bich, what the assfuk are you yapping about this time?" snapped Crump, as he gave the Crump House press secretary the fukeye.

"Bubba and the Flyin Possums, Mr. President," whooped Bich, while dancing around the Resolute desk. "They're the number one country band in the whole of fukkin Arkansas."

"Goddamnit, Bich, I hope you're not going to tell me that these Southern fukkers are Rusty Beaver's replacement," retorted Crump, as he turned to me and shook his head.

"I sure am, Mr. President," grinned Bich, yet again. "I've got the contract right here. They're born again Crumpers and converts to Crumpism. So they've agreed to sing at the openin' of ya pyramid for a jug of Granny's homemade hooch and a seat at the hog roast I'm organisin' afterward."

"Bich, you're a fukaholic, you know that," shouted Crump,

while throwing a half-eaten Crumpburger at the Crump House press secretary. "And why the fuk are they called the Flyin Possums?"

"Well, Mr. President, back in Arkansas, Bubba's fans like to throw live possums onto the stage while the band's performin'. So that's how they got their name," explained Bich, who happened to be one of their biggest fans.

Flyin possums aside, that night, I barely slept a wink as my head was filled with thoughts of the historic and no doubt memorable day that lay ahead. When I eventually dragged myself out of bed the following morning, I pulled on my best business suit before leaving my room in nearby Foggy Bottom. Opening the Oval Office door at just after 11 am, I was surprised to see Crump with his feet on the Resolute desk, as in my experience, leading the free world rarely got underway before noon.

Following a leisurely two-hour lunch of Crumpburgers and diet coke with the newly appointed Vice President of the United States, the three of us, along with Asyphilis, left the Crump House for a short ride in the Beast. Naturally, we were not alone, as a sizeable presidential motorcade accompanied us to convey almost every member of the Crump House staff and the Secret Service to the Crump Monument. However, this did not include the current residents of the Crump House dungeon, who would have to make do with watching the day's festivities on a small wall-mounted television.

As the presidential motorcade approached the National Mall, at long last, I could see the colossal Crump Monument in its entire imposing splendor. Not only did it better the old Washington Monument by a good 100 feet, but at its base, it was easily the size of two football fields. With its North Korean grey granite exterior and red Crumpburger neon signs on each of its four sides, the pyramid's apex was topped off with a 24 Karat gold statue of Crump. And this, to my awe, must have reached another 50 feet towards the heavens.

A stand had been erected some 100 yards in front of the pyramid, and this was reserved for Crump et al. and his paying guests from the ranks of the rich and famous. Because the presidential election was only days away, Crump also permitted a standing-only section at the foot of the Crump Monument for what he termed the dickstrapped poor. Though it should have come as no surprise to any of them, admittance was dependent on completing a mail-in ballot with a vote for Crump in the presence of a Crump House official.

Once we had exited the Beast, our first port of call was the 3,000 capacity Crumpburger at the heart of the pyramid. In addition to our party of four, we were accompanied by Bich Landers and Oleander OnYurway. And with their cameras rolling, all three of the SHITE buddies and the fukkers in the fake press were present to air the awe-inspiring event live. As Crump was keen to get the cash registers ringing, he wasted no time at all in cutting the ribbon before declaring the largest Crumpburger in the world open for business.

After answering the typical congratulatory asslicking question that Vaj Ingersol always liked to ask, he gave short shrift to the dumbass questions posed by the fukkers in the fake press. Moving on, Crump, Asyphilis, Tribianka, and I left Bich and OnYurway with the Crump House press corps to seek a private audience with Archbishop Dwight Jacoff. And although I was thrilled to be one of the first to visit the Church of Crump, I have to admit, I felt a little underwhelmed by the seat of Crumpism, which turned out to be no more than an office full of bean counters and a rather large safe.

We scarcely spent ten minutes with the Archbishop, who tried to play the part by dousing us with diet coke, as this was Crumpism's answer to holy water. Crump, though, appeared to be pleased with Crumpburger's Vice President of Quality. This was because conversions to Crumpism were progressing as planned, and most religious places of worship had now been dissolved and their buildings converted to Crumpburgers. And on top of that, religious dispensations, particularly those concerning downloading porn, were bringing in a shitload of cash.

As time was marching on, we exited the Crump Monument and were met by a dozen Secret Service agents who escorted us to our seats to await the commencement of the afternoon's official proceedings. It was then I could see we were in good hands that day as not only were the Secret Service out in force, but Bich had arranged for 2,000 armed Arkansas National Guardsmen to be there as well.

Facing the pyramid in pride of place on the uppermost row of the stand, I was seated to the left of Crump with Asyphilis to his right, while Tribianka, as always, sat on Crump's lap. Directly in front of us were Bich and OnYurway, and sitting next to them were Vaj Ingersol, Dicker Polson, and a muzzled Ranting Prick Enderbee. The fukkers in the fake press were not so lucky in their choice of seating though, as they had been placed, at Crump's request, in a fenced-off enclosure at ground level.

"Hey, Crump, so you spent a billion dollars of taxpayers' money for a rocket to hit that private members-only club of yours. And now I hear you're spending more of our hard-earned money to rebuild the fukkin thing," shouted Loudmouth

Lonnie Laverty of SBC, who had recovered from his injury sustained in the fukkers briefing room and was now standing in the enclosure with the other members of the fake press. "So does that mean we'll all be members of Kiss-my-Ass now?"

Unfortunately for Loudmouth, his wisecracking was short-lived that afternoon, because, without any hesitation, OnYurway pulled out one of her magnums and shot the fukker. This sent Dillard Wowser into a hysterical fit of screaming, and that was all it took for the Arkansas National Guard to throw tear gas and flash-bang grenades into the enclosure. Disappointingly for many of us watching from the stand, it seemed like the altercation was over before it really got started as within minutes the Park Police had arrested and carted off each and every one of the fukkers, much to Crump's amusement.

"Possum anyone," called out Bich, as she turned around with a live possum in one hand and a cage containing another five in the other. "I told Granny that Bubba and the Flyin Possums would be playin' today, so she sent me half a dozen possums for us to throw at Bubba and the rest of the band when they're on stage."

While Tribianka, Asyphilis, and I simply shook our heads, Crump turned to me and rolled his eyes before muttering the words, "Arkansas nutjob." Consequently, Bich handed a possum to OnYurway, and three more to each of the SHITE buddies, which pleased the Crump House press secretary no end because that meant she would be able to throw the two remaining possums herself.

According to the program I held in my hand, Archbishop Dwight Jacoff was to bless the Crump Monument immediately after the US Air Force's aerial display. Once the impressive testament to Crump's vanity was officially open, we were to be rewarded with a rendition of Crump is Simply the Best by Bubba and the Flyin Possums. This was to be followed by a selection of their hit songs, the words of which, Bich claimed, were well known to everyone, as long as they were from Arkansas. Then to round the afternoon off, a North Korean style military parade, just like the one Crump had seen in Pyongyang, was to be held on Constitution Avenue. And this would feature just about every weapon of mass destruction, including a sizeable part of the US nuclear arsenal, known to man.

At three on the dot, a roar was heard, and then a squadron of military jets flew by to signal the start of the US Air Force's tribute to Crump. Then high above our heads they soared before commencing an aerial bombardment of the Democratic National Committee headquarters. As everyone around us got to their feet and clapped, a laughing Crump turned to me and uttered, "That'll teach the fukkers," just as each of the pilots saluted their commander in chief in a fly by that ended with them crashing into the Potomac, which, I suspected, was not meant to be part of the show.

Now that the afternoon had started with a bang, Archbishop Dwight Jacoff appeared at the entrance to the Crump Monument and raised his arms in the air to silence the animated crowd before him. Wearing a Crumpburger cap and his robes of office, which featured a Crumpburger logo on the front and back, he gracefully ascended the pyramid with the aid of one of those stairlifts that are typically the favorite of old fukkers. Then being that idolatry was an intrinsic part of Crumpism, the Archbishop knelt at the foot of the 24 Karat gold statue of Crump. And that's where, while spouting a whole load of asinine shit, a member of his flock recorded the ceremony and streamed it in real-time so that we could view the remarkable event on our phones.

"Bubba and the Flyin possums are gonna be on next, Mr. President," hollered Bich, who was now holding a possum in each hand, ready to throw. "That sure was a shitdinger of a speech by the Archbishop. Even those dead fukkers would have appreciated it."

"What dead fukkers? Bich, have you been drinking Twatt Jabowsky's moonshine again?" demanded Crump, as he looked at me and shook his head, and then silently mouthed the words, "Fukkin loopy."

"The dead mad fukkers, Mr. President. There must be a million or more of 'em buried in that there pyramid," replied Bich, with a grin.

Even though the Crump Monument was beyond a shadow of a doubt an enormous structure, I was sure it could not possibly accommodate the bodies of so many lost souls. And besides, it housed the Church of Crump and a 3,000 seat Crumpburger, which, I pointed out to the Crump House press secretary, meant she must be mistaken. Then Crump nodded his head, and in his own inimitable way, reminded me that everyone from Arkansas was fukkin asscrazy.

"Mr. President, I ain't been drinkin', or gone fukeroo on ya, like when Granny thought she was a prairie dog and spent a year livin' in a tree," retorted Bich, who looked a little riled with us. "I had them mad fukkers cremated because Cooter told me people's ashes are no different than fukkin cement. It saved us millions, I can tell ya, but the overseers from the Secret Service still charged the US Treasury for the real thing. So all them mad fukkers are really buried in ya dickass pyramid, just like I said, only they're in the mortar that binds every one of the million mothafukkin bricks."

As it happened, before any of us could say another word, the crowd began to clap as Bubba and the Flyin Possums staggered onto the wooden stage at the foot of the Crump Monument. Clearly bladdered, due to drinking too much of Granny Landers homemade hooch, they waved to us, and then Bubba launched into the band's Countrified take on Crump is Simply the Best.

By the time the Flyin Possums had joined in, Crump's signature tune was loudly resonating from the band's oversized speakers mounted on the side of the pyramid. It was then that I felt the first of a series of inconsequential ground tremors seemingly originating from the Crump Monument. At first, I thought nothing of them, as my mentor did not look concerned in the least. Instead, I leaned back in my seat to enjoy the once-in-a-lifetime spectacle of seeing six screeching possums fly through the air towards the stage.

At that point in the show, the tremors grew more violent, and panicked shrieks of EARTHQUAKE! FUKKIN EARTHQUAKE could be heard. And then several Secret Service agents grabbed Crump and his Vice President by the arms and whisked them away to the emergency exit at the rear of the stand. As they had left Asyphilis and me behind to face whatever catastrophe was coming, I caught hold of the First Lady's hand and hurriedly followed the others. Then as we reached the safety of the Beast, it was plain to see what was happening as the mighty Crump Monument came crashing to the ground.

Upon our return to the Crump House, while Tribianka and I sat on the sofa drinking diet coke, uncharacteristically, a fuming Crump paced up and down the Oval Office. With the military parade now canceled and his pyramid no more than a pile of rubble, he held Bick Landers personally responsible for what had become the latest in a long line of monumental fukups. So it was quite a surprise to us all to hear someone tapping at the window. And that someone turned out to be the Crump House press secretary, grinning with one of her thumb's in the air.

Without having to be asked, I walked over to the window and opened it so that Bich could climb in. As Crump gave her the fukeye, she dusted herself off, and that was when I noticed a long military vehicle parked on the South Lawn. As I gazed at it for a second or two, I realized it was one of the missile carriers that would have been part of Crump's military parade. Strangely, though, I could see the 50 foot 24 Karat gold statue of Crump that had stood on top of the Crump Monument was now chained to the solitary nuclear warhead it had been hauling.

"That sure was an asscracker of a show, Mr. President, and I have to say, it was probably their best yet," said Bich, with a grin. Although she failed to mention that it had been Bubba and the Flyin Possums last. "And there's no need to worry ya ass off about that pyramid because I called Cooter and he reckons it'll be fukkin easy to repair. But for safekeepin', I had the Arkansas National Guard retrieve that big ol' shitbanger of a statue, so no thievin' fukweasel will be able to get their hands on it. They strapped it to one of them goddamn fuksticks on the back of a vehicle the army boys were drivin', and then I drove it back to the Crump House myself. If ya give me a minute, I'll reverse it into the Rose Garden and park the fukker next to ya anti-aircraft gun."

"Bich, it was a total fukfest. And it was all because you had the assbrained idea of using cremated mad fukkers instead of regular cement," yelled Crump, as he sat down on his chair at the Resolute desk. "You know, if OnYurway was here, I'd have her shoot you in the head with one of her magnums in a dicksneeze."

"Daddy, can we put her on the rack?" squealed Tribianka, who was referring to the medieval torture rack that had been installed in the Crump House dungeon the day before.

"Of course, anything for Daddy's little girl," nodded Crump, with a smile. Then there was a knock on the door, and in walked a disheveled Oleander OnYurway. "Ah, at last, OnYurway, escort Bich to the dungeon, and though it'll be a squeeze, lock her up with those other two fukkers. Oh yes, and if she gives you any trouble, shoot her in the fukkin head."

"Mr. President, but what about the goddamn hog roast?" wailed Bich, as OnYurway dragged her out of the Oval Office kicking and screaming all the way to the Crump House dungeon.

With Bich Landers residing in the Crump House dungeon, the next few days were some of the quietest of my yearlong presidential internship. Along with countless games of Twister, most of our afternoon working hours were spent watching SHITE news shitwag about how Crump was going to win the election by a landslide. Twatt Jabowsky and Skeeter Shiznit, meanwhile, were working closely with the Republican National Committee to mail in fraudulent ballots for Crump. And the rest of the Crump House team were as busy as bees placing fake ballot drop-off boxes in Democrat-leaning areas to ensure their votes would never be counted.

Having a front-row seat to witness American democracy at its finest was undeniably an illuminating experience for me. And one that I knew would stand me in good stead to pursue a political career back in England. While I couldn't vote myself without purchasing a fake ID, in the final days before the election I rooted for Crump as best I could. And this not only meant I wrote Crump's shit-stirring tweets, but I also helped him with a patriotic call to ASS men to intimidate likely Fudrucker voters at polling stations throughout the country.

As Crump needed every vote he could legally get his hands on and more, on Election Day, he authorized the release of the three detainees in the Crump House dungeon. Just like Asyphilis and Tribianka and every other registered flag-waving Republican, they voted as many times as they could. Then not to be outdone, with the help of Skeeter Shiznit's associates, Crump cast a vote for himself in every one of the 48 states of the Union.

While Election Day started well enough with the SHITE buddies declaring Crump the victor even before polling stations had opened, unfortunately, exit polls across the country painted a very different picture. Every so often, Bich Landers, who was now a good inch taller after being stretched on the rack in the Crump House dungeon, dropped by the Oval Office to give us the bad news. By late afternoon, not only had Crump received next to no votes in the shitster Democratic states, but alarmingly, he was behind in the sure bet Crumper states as well.

Undaunted, Crump appeared on SHITE news to declare exit polls were just dickbeating fukery concocted by the fukkers in the fake press. Then he went on to retweet a slew of shit by unnamed sources claiming Smilin' Mo Fudrucker was dead. It was certainly a nail-biting time for most of us in the Crump House, and it didn't help that counting electoral ballots in the US of A turned out to be slower than an old fukker climbing the stairs. Though oddly enough, I couldn't help but notice that Crump looked supremely confident throughout the entire nerve-racking day.

It wasn't until the following week when most of the ballots had been counted, that the fake press announced Smilin' Mo

Fudrucker was the winner. Unperturbed, with the support of SHITE news and the stalwarts of the Republican Party, Crump made an address to the nation claiming he had won by a dickswinging mile. Then as thousands of gun-toting ASS men poured into the nation's capital to enforce their constitutional right to mutiny, the Crump-appointed Supreme Court ruled that winning a US presidential election don't mean shit. And so in the final days of my presidential internship, I sat in the Oval Office with a triumphant Crump, as he tweeted out, Fukkers – Crump wins again!

"Well, Trenton, the election is over, so I guess you'll be returning to England soon, which leaves me on my lonesome with a bunch of fukheaded assmonkeys," sighed Crump, as he shook his head and then handed me a can of diet coke. "Now, don't forget what you've learned over the past year, and when you get back home, stick it to the fukkers and make England great again."

"Make England Great Again. You know, Crump, that has a nice ring to it," I told him, as I opened my notepad for the last time in the Oval Office and jotted down the word, MEGA.